Me and Mr. G
(And Various Side Trips)

by

Mary C. Meglemre

As Told To Mary C. Meglemre

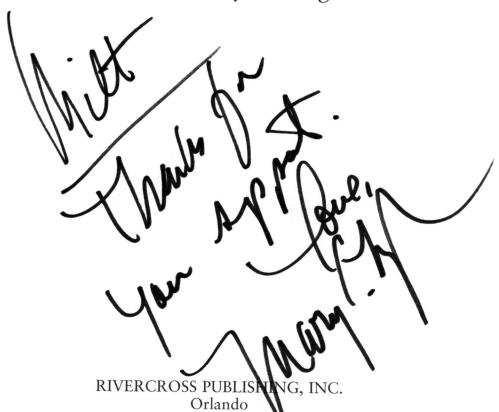

RIVERCROSS PUBLISHING, INC.
Orlando

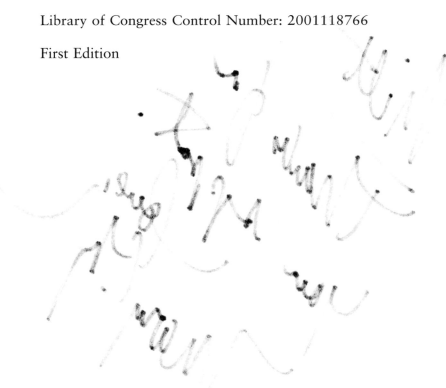

DEDICATION

To E

From Me

Introduction

As I grow older, I realize I must sit in one place and write my story. Well, at least the interesting parts.

I have wrestled with myself over the importance of my life story, but the people who know me the best have convinced me that my life truly is unique.

To say my life took more turns than a grand prix race is an understatement—trainer, jockey, actress, impersonator, bodyguard, bounty hunter, confidante, and writer. I always believed that to live your life to the fullest . . . was to find as many lives to fill. My trips were sometimes rocky, but more often than not, they were full of wonder and fulfillment.

The parade of people I have already met would fill the pages of the National Enquirer 'till the year 2050. I don't doubt for one minute that pages from this book will find their way to the N.E.'s front pages. Hell, if they are so fast to print trash about the people in this book, maybe this time they'll print the truth.

Me and Mr. G opens the door to a man who was, above all, a loving father and a great friend. The world of horse racing was not opened to me in the beginning. But, because of my "head down, butt up" approach, I was able to work for one of the best barns in the world.

La Cage was the most interesting stop on my lives' journeys. To play a man—playing a woman—playing Judy Garland, was a true actor's dream. To this day I don't believe people knew what was under my skirt. At times I had to check for myself to make sure who I was.

Hunting humans was the most challenging. To be part animal, part human, and part criminal, made this chapter the most important job I have ever done.

The following will not be a journalistic masterpiece. I could have easily dedicated this book to Bob Joyce, the editor who got the unenviable job of checking my grammar and spelling and had to make sense out of some of my ramblings.

Also, I warn you to take whatever you read in the following pages with a grain of salt. You see, when I relay stories, I sometimes get carried away. Thus, the stories end up sounding bigger and better than they really are, especially when the stories make me look good.

So, grab your socks and hold on—it's asses and elbows from here on!

ENJOY!

Mary C. Meglemre
Paramount, California
June 2001

Me and Mr. G
(and various side trips)

The following was inspired by the latest book written about Cary Grant, a 300-plus-page coffee table book addressing such burning questions as: "Was he gay? Did he do drugs? Did he beat his wives?; Could he be trusted with farm animals?" If that is the way you want to remember this bigger-than-life giant of the silver screen, then close this book, put it down, and walk away.

Also, since I don't know it all, this isn't a "Tell all Book." Still reading? Then sit back and enjoy a story about a loving father and loyal friend. Later on, I tell how Me and Mr. G's life paths crossed.

I don't want to give the impression that Mr. G and I were bosom buddies. While I was his employee, it was all business. We finally became close friends after his beloved Jennifer went off to college. But the bond between us was first formed when Mr. G asked me why I called him Mr. G, instead of Cary Grant. I explained to him that the first time I saw him and his daughter together, he became

Mr. G, Jennifer's daddy. This touched him very much, and from that point on we were close.

The only personal question I think I ever asked Mr. G was how hard it was being Cary Grant. He said being Cary Grant was easy; being Archie Leach was impossible. I knew with that answer that his childhood was probably not a happy one. So I worked very hard to make sure Jennifer had a normal childhood. I did whatever I could to keep the outside from coming in. I took Jennifer to the Santa Monica pier where we would ride the carousel for hours, and the time spent with the horses was quality time.

Jennifer's mother, Dyan Cannon, was a different story. Until she writes her own book (suggested title, The Day I Became a Broodmare)*, she won't be able to chase her demons away. To this day, I know she still has a lot of problems because of her life with Cary Grant. I know Jennifer now understands her mother and forgives her. The past was full of so much anger and resentment. Thank God, Dyan had the Lakers, and Jennifer had me. I hope when Dyan writes her book, she puts in a chapter about one Lakers star in particular . . . she could call it* The First Switch-hitting Basketball Player.

On any given day or night, Mr. G's house was open to the royalty of Hollywood and the top CEOs of the business world. One such person was Grace Kelly, the Princess of Monaco. Mr. G felt guilty when she died. He knew what was going on in the palace, and because he was the one who introduced Grace to his Royal Highness Prince Rainier, a person I found to lack compassion and manners. As a matter of fact, he wanted to crown Marilyn Monroe as his Princess of Monaco. That alone should tell you what kind of man he was. Also, that should have tipped you off as to how much he really loved Grace. Later on, in royal history, another loveless marriage played out and another princess wound up dying way too young.

His country was close to bankruptcy, so the Prince and his subjects needed a fairy tale to put some life back into the tiny seaside resort. Mr. G stepped in, and the rest is history. Never mind that Grace was in love with someone else, or that she never liked the Prince. The country was about to drop into the ocean, never to be seen again.

As time went by, Mr. G got Grace involved in the business world as a board member of MGM. That way, Grace could leave the palace and there would not be any rumors. While

8

visiting the U.S. for her children's charities, she would also be meeting her former lover, Oleg Cassini. That was her escape. Mr. G arranged most of the meetings, and that eased his conscience. In the end, Grace did not die on that mountain. She died years before in a church beside a man she knew never loved her.

One former friend Mr. G was disappointed in was Sophia Loren. When Ms. Loren was going through her financial troubles, she did the only thing she could do—she wrote a book. In the book, she lied about having a sexual relationship with Mr. G (while filming the movie *Houseboat*). This hurt him very much because he was happily married to Betsy Drake at the time.

I was at the house when he called Ms. Loren. She told him she never wanted to hurt him or his wife. She said the people who talked her into writing the book said she would have to lie to make it interesting. Mr. G's response was that if she needed the money that badly, she could have come to him. I believe that was the last time they spoke.

One very special lady in Mr. G's life was Greta ("I want to be alone") Garbo. Few people knew that this timeless beauty and Mr. G had real estate holdings together. I had a hard time believing one story Mr. G told me. Since I could not find any real evidence to back up this vindictive tale, I wrote the following fictional short story, called "Lucinda." After reading it, I hope you come away with the same feeling I had. One woman gave up a career for love, and the other gave up love for a career. To this day, I don't know who was the happiest in the end. But I'm sure of one thing—when Garbo left Hollywood the heavens gave up their brightest star, never to be replaced.

Lucinda

Being T.J. Lang's assistant for twenty years was never easy, but it was always full of surprises. This particular afternoon held the biggest surprise of my long tenure with the legendary director, writer, and producer. I was suddenly out of work!

Here, in the emergency room of Cedar-Sinai Hospital in Beverly Hills, his heart had betrayed him. After years of abuse, I really couldn't blame it.

The E.R. physician entered the waiting room.

"Is there anyone with the patient who was just brought in?"

"Yes, I'm Mary Steward, Mr. Lang's assistant. I brought him in. Do you need some information for his admission?"

I could see in the doctor's face that admission was not on his mind.

"No. What I need is a family member or next of kin." Then it hit me. T.J. was either dead or close to it. Yet, somehow it didn't sink in and I reacted as if I was just handling another piece of routine business for my boss.

"Well, I guess since I'm his executor, as well as his assistant, I would have to qualify for his next of kin. I don't believe he has any relatives."

He really didn't. I knew that he was an only child. His mother died when he was a boy and his father passed away a few years later. He was raised by an old friend of his parents who had also long since passed away. Besides, this all happened in his native Sweden.

"Then I guess I should give you the bad news. Mr. Lang never regained consciousness after a massive heart attack. I'm sorry. We worked on him and did everything we could to save him. His heart just gave out."

It was like I was listening to the doctor's words through a tunnel, the strange echoing sound filling my head. Worse, it sounded like some dialogue from one of T.J.'s own scripts. You see, working for T.J. all of these years made it hard to recognize the difference between real life and the life he created on the screen.

"Well, Mr. Lang's heart has been a problem for the last few years, and I guess this was to be expected," I said. "I know you tried your best, but as Mr. Lang would say, 'When it's a wrap, it's a wrap.'"

The young emergency room doctor broke into a smile at my response. His burden was lifted a little. He obviously was new at delivering bad news, and was feeling the loss right along with me. After a few more months as an E.R. physician, it would come a lot easier.

✳ ✳ ✳ ✳ ✳

Two days later while trying to sort through the enormous amount of unfinished business on T.J.'s desk, his long-time personal attorney, Brad Casey, called and announced that he'd be by shortly. I assumed it had to do with settling the estate, but it turned out that Casey was merely a courier that day.

"Hello, Mary. How are you doing?"

"I'm doing okay, but it's going to take quite some time to go through his papers."

"Well, I guess I'm going to add to your paperwork," Casey said. "About a month ago, T.J. handed me a sealed envelope with explicit instructions to give it to you, and only you, upon his death."

"A month ago?" I asked. "That seems strange. Did he say he was sick, or thought he might die?"

11

"Not a word. He might have suspected something, but he looked fine and said nothing about his health."

"And you didn't ask what it was?"

"Mary, I'm an attorney. I do a lot of unusual, sometimes strange things for my clients. And you know T.J. was as unique as they come. He paid me well, so I didn't ask."

He took an envelope out of his inside suit pocket. "He knew you'd be here at his desk about now and asked me to personally deliver the envelope. He did say that it was a job you needed to do after he died, and that you'd need some documents I kept in an office safe for him."

"Good old T.J., always a flair for the dramatic and a master of timing. Well, let's see what the old guy still has up his sleeve." Brad handed me a sealed envelope. "Do you want to wait around while I read it?"

"Not at all," Brad replied. "In fact, T.J. made it clear to me that you were to be the only one to read it."

Brad left. I dropped into T.J.'s oversized desk chair, opened the envelope and began to read.

✵ ✵ ✵ ✵ ✵

Mary, my dear Mary. I know you must be feeling lonely now, since I was your only reason for living.

One sentence, and I was already getting angry. How dare he think I had such a dull life that he was the only person in it. A few seconds of honest reflection, however, turned my anger toward myself. His words rang true. I thought about my life, and he was right. Other than an occasional night out with the girls, I had no life.

When T.J. hired me twenty years earlier, he warned me that the entertainment business would consume me. I gave little thought to that advice then, but now the years had proven his comment only too true.

There had been no burning love affairs, no meeting strangers in strange places. I didn't even have any family ties to speak of anymore. After turning down so many holiday and birthday invitations, they finally gave me up for dead.

So, T.J. was right. With him gone, what was I going to do? I continued reading his letter.

But rest assured, your employment is not yet at an end. I have one last duty for you to perform.

You know more about my business and my personal life than anyone else in the world. But although I shared almost everything with you, I was bound by yet another, older friendship to keep a secret throughout my lifetime. I now have reason to believe that my time is short, so I need to reveal events that occurred a very long time ago and ask you to rectify a terrible wrong.

In the early 1950s, one of the world's greatest stars left the heavens. Her name was Lucinda. I had discovered this radiant child on one of my visits to France. She was in a local pageant, some small town festival, celebrating something or another. She was sitting on the back of a horse cart, just smiling. As a matter of fact, I didn't hear her speak until later that night.

Just seeing her smile told me so much about who she was. I didn't care how she sounded.

I was later blessed when I found out she had a voice that was as alluring as her smile. I had already made up my mind that I wanted to sign her, but I'd have to use small town protocol. I knew I would have to approach a family member to get any information about her. Her father turned out to be a very agreeable "agent," and we soon struck a deal.

Six months later, Lucinda was in Hollywood. Everything I saw in this lovely girl was true, and the camera saw what I saw and more. She was a true natural talent. With a beautiful face, gorgeous body and sensuous voice, Lucinda had all the makings of a star. The movie-going public soon fell in love with Lucinda.

Then, one day, she asked me to meet her somewhere to talk. This upset me. We had worked together for almost two years and made five pictures. During that time, she never spoke of anything but work. But I felt she now needed to tell me something that she had kept inside for a long time. I set up the meeting in my office, on the lot, so it would go unnoticed and she would feel more comfortable.

When she entered the office, I knew she was troubled. "Lucinda. Please sit down. Can I get you anything?" She silently waved away my offer.

"Well, what's on your mind, my friend?" I asked.

Her voice was barely audible. I had to lean over my desk to hear her.

"When you came to my town and asked me to leave and make films, I was hesitant to do this. My reasons you will never understand. But I feel you have the right to know why I am having a change of heart now.

13

"I was 18 years old when you came to my town. One year earlier, I had fallen in love. This love has not left my heart. As hard as I've tried, it pulls me back to my home with a power I can't fight."

Knowing Lucinda, I knew nothing in her life was done half-heartedly, so I believed every word she said and felt her pain. She was truly hurting, but I figured that maybe I could help the young actress solve her love problem.

"Can't you bring this guy to Hollywood and make your life together here? Or is he one of these men who doesn't want a working wife?"

She looked up from her hands neatly folded in her lap. "I don't think my work would be a problem," she replied. "The problem would come from people not accepting that my lover is a woman."

My heart stopped. My brain raced to find the words to send to my mouth so I wouldn't say the wrong thing.

"Are you saying that your lover is a woman? Does this mean you're a lesbian?" This was the kind of question Lucinda would expect me to ask—direct and to the point. I knew it would not offend her.

"If that's what you want to call it. I only know I feel this love for this woman. And I know I cannot go on with my life without her."

"Worse secrets than this have been kept behind closed doors in this town," I offered, "and no one was the wiser. I don't think this is a problem."

She shifted forward in her chair, anticipating that I might actually have a solution for the situation she considered so grave.

"Would it bother you if I put out the story that your friend was really a cousin who wanted to move to the U.S.?"

"If it would fill both of our needs, I will consent to it." After discussing the details of getting her friend to California, Lucinda left my office, and not another word was said.

Two weeks passed and then Lilly, Lucinda's younger "cousin," arrived. They could easily have passed for cousins, even sisters. Lilly was a mirror image of Lucinda, except not quite as strikingly beautiful.

Lilly, I was to find out, was a very talented artist, having already been shown in galleries all over Europe. Lucinda had brought some of Lilly's work with her when she came to Hollywood. I was always struck by its beauty. Little did I know, Lucinda was Lilly's inspiration.

A year passed. Lucinda and Lilly were living their lives in private—just another well-kept Hollywood secret. No one *ever suspected that one of Hollywood's true goddesses (which she had by then become), was deeply and happily in love with a woman.*

Lucinda's work improved with every movie. She was gaining more and more confidence in her acting style. There was no doubt in my mind that much of it was due to the fact that Lilly was now with her. They had this incredible way of supporting each other.

A writer friend called and said he had finished his book, Daybreak, and wanted to know if I would be interested in reading it. "Send it over," I told him, "I'll take it to Palm Springs." When I read it, I realized that it was a good book and had a great part for Lucinda.

I called her from the "Springs," and told her the good news. We were both excited because we had gone through a disappointing stretch where we couldn't seem to find any decent scripts for her. And Lucinda was getting cabin fever without a new role.

It didn't take long for word of this super script to reach the studios. My phone was soon ringing off the hook. Two actresses called and asked if they could read for the part. I told both Elizabeth Davidson and Joan Palmer that the part had been cast.

Elizabeth Davidson took the news very hard. "T.J., I hate to beg, but I really need a good part now. I think the studio is losing interest in me."

"That's crazy talk, Liz. You've never been better. Your last movies were great box office. And I hear Metro is trying to deal for your services."

I was trying to be kind. The truth was, good women's parts were becoming fewer and fewer. As a matter of fact, if this new script hadn't come along, I would have had trouble finding work for Lucinda.

"Well, I guess calling you for the part was a dumb idea anyhow," Liz continued. "Everything you produce is always for your precious little Parisian princess."

I sensed Liz "The Cat" Davidson was about to uncoil her very sharp claws. "Now Liz, don't start throwing mud. You know Lucinda is very talented."

"I know, but lately she's been taking more than her share of the good parts. I think she should go on vacation for a couple of years and give some of us other ladies a chance. Better yet, she should find a man and have about a dozen kids."

She paused, and I anticipated what followed.

15

"Speaking of men, why hasn't your girl been dating? I hear from some gentlemen friends of mine that when they ask her out, she says no. Could it be your little love goddess is a cold fish?" I had to bite my tongue on that one.

Little did Liz know that Lucinda and Lilly logged more hours in bed than Liz and all of her so-called lovers combined. And I would bet the quality of passion in Lucinda's bed had to be better than in Liz's. I always figured Liz couldn't come even if you called her.

"Now, Liz, just because Lucinda doesn't bed hop around town doesn't mean she's a cold fish."

"Oh, T.J., I didn't say I believed all those rumors. I just find it hard to believe she doesn't have a man in her life—I mean, besides you, dear."

"Well, Liz, I've got to get to work. Thanks for calling and we'll do lunch soon. Love to everyone over at Metro."

Joan Palmer was more of a lady.

"Hi, T.J. This is Joan. I heard you have a great script on your desk. Is there any chance I could read for the part?"

I always respected Joan for her directness, and it really upset me to have to tell her the part had been cast.

"Well, you can't knock a girl for trying. By the way, tell Lucinda good luck. I know she'll be great."

Good ol' Joan. She knew Lucinda was my choice, but tried anyway. If I had never found Lucinda, Joan would be my star. And, God forbid, if anything happened to Lucinda, I would have given the part to Joan.

Everything was in place, and the movie started shooting. Lucinda's performance was inspiring. Every scene she was in had her mark on it. Halfway through the shoot, I knew Lucinda would get an invite to that "Monday in March."

A year later, Lucinda and I both showed up for that Monday in March and left with a couple of statues. Best Director and Best Actress Oscars were our rewards for the blood, sweat, and tears we both gave.

I told Lucinda to take some time off, maybe go home to France for a visit. She said that Lilly and she were talking about going south to Mexico.

"That's a great idea," I said. "See you when you get back."

Two months went by. I was in my office when my phone rang. It was Lucinda.

"Hello, T.J."

"Hello," I replied. "How was your vacation?"

Her voice was not happy. She simply said, "Please come up to the house as soon as you can. I'll give you the directions."

I was caught completely off guard. In all of the years I'd known Lucinda, this was the first time she'd invited me to the place she shared with Lilly.

It turned out to be a two-story house in the Hollywood hills. I think it must have been bought for Lilly because the surroundings were so inspiring for an artist.

Lilly greeted me at the door. "Hello, T.J. Come in. Lucinda's expecting you."

I followed Lilly down a flight of steps to a sunken living room, where Lucinda was sitting on a couch near the fireplace.

She looked up at me and tried to smile, but could not. Her eyes looked back into the fire.

"Can I get you a drink?" Lilly asked.

"Yes, some white wine would be nice."

Lilly left the room, and I sat in a chair across from Lucinda.

"What's up? You look troubled."

Her eyes searched the room, trying to find the words she needed to say. Finally our eyes met.

"I have something to show you," she said at last. Out of a large envelope she pulled a typewritten note and handed it to me.

Dear Competition,
Get your lesbian ass out of Hollywood or I'll send these pictures to the papers.
Someone who knows.

Then Lucinda reached back into the envelope and removed a photo of Lucinda and Lilly kissing and embracing. They were topless. From the background, it was obvious the picture was taken at their beach house in Mexico.

Lilly returned with my wine and sat next to Lucinda.

"Lilly and I didn't invite you up here to help us make a decision. We've already done that. We want you to know our decision and give you time to make up a story about my departure."

"Are you really ready to give up everything because of this blackmailing S.O.B.?" I asked.

"In Europe, Lilly and I can live in a more open relationship. Hiding would never suit us, and hiding is what we would have to do here."

17

I knew I would never change their minds. Lilly put her arm on Lucinda's shoulder and finished the conversation for her lover who could no longer talk.

"We are grateful for all you've done for us," Lilly said, "but we have chosen to stay together, and that's impossible here."

In less than one month, Lucinda and Lilly were gone. And so was a very large part of my life.

I didn't realize how much these two women meant to me. Their love for each other had always given me a warm feeling. And, God knows, in this business that feeling doesn't come often.

Now, my dear Mary, this is where you come in. You now know the story. I want you to find out who blackmailed Lucinda. As of the time of my passing, all parties were still alive. Brad Casey, my lawyer, has all of the numbers and addresses of everyone involved.

When you've completed your task, you will receive your inheritance and your last paycheck.

My dearest Mary, I'm sorry I never told you how much you meant to me. After losing Lucinda and Lilly, I never thought I could be happy. But you made my life worth living. For 20 years, you never once said no. You hung in there with me through some tough times and never complained once. The time we spent together was all too short.

You were truly everything to me. The only thing I hate about the idea of dying is how much I will miss you!

Good luck, Mary. I know you'll solve this mystery. You must!

One woman gave up love for a career, and another gave up a career for love. Both women need to know. They've both paid a big price for their actions. They deserve to know.

Mary, my dearest,
T.J.

* * * * *

I felt as if I had just run in a marathon. I was exhausted and a bit bewildered. I knew about Lucinda of course. The entire world knew about Lucinda, the great actress who abruptly left Hollywood to live a secretive life in Europe.

I knew T.J. had brought her to this country and had been responsible for igniting her career. Yet, I knew there was much he didn't or wouldn't tell me. Like Casey, there were things I didn't ask Lang.

I never knew he had these feelings. And on top of everything, I now had to deal with his feelings for me.

For the first time, I truly felt the loss. T.J. would never again show up at my place in the middle of the night with an idea that just couldn't wait, or have me suddenly drive him to Santa Barbara and back to work out some pitch he had to present.

Life without T.J. Well, maybe if I take a long time solving the Lucinda mystery it will still be like working for him.

The next day, I went to Brad Casey's office to pick up all of the information T.J. left for me. There were two additional sealed envelopes with my name on them.

"T.J. said you'd need these," Casey said. "Knowing T.J., whatever job he left for you—it must really be special."

"What makes you think that?" I asked as if I had been assigned nothing special.

"Here's why." Brad handed me a check in my name for one million dollars! "When that runs out, there's more. T.J. left an open account. Your money is almost endless!"

I was in shock. What in Heaven's name would cost a million dollars? A payoff here and there couldn't cost so much money. Then again, maybe T.J. knew more about payoffs than I do.

Another flash hit me. Why would T.J. think I'd know how to track down a blackmailer? Maybe he knew me better than I know myself.

After getting back to the house, I sat down and went through all of the paperwork. Before I knew it, I found a very neat puzzle in front of me. There were many clues in this intricate maze, and they were beginning to fall into place. T.J. had all but left me a map.

First, was it a man or a woman? It had to be a woman ("Dear Competition"). Maybe a fellow actress. Besides, men call gay women dykes, not lesbians. Since T.J. was only contacted by two women (Joan Palmer and Elizabeth Davidson), it had to be one of them. Or was this simply too obvious. It could have been almost anyone in jealousy-infested Hollywood!

I decided to start with the two most likely suspects. A call to Liz Davidson surprisingly produced a meeting the very next day.

A very large man came to the door at Davidson's mansion. "Yes, may I help you?"

"My name is Mary Steward, and I have an appointment with Miss Davidson."

"This way, please."

I followed the giant into a living room and waited for my suspect.

"Hello, I'm Liz Davidson. And you're Mary Steward, right?"

"Yes." I knew of Davidson professionally, but we had never actually met. She was no longer active on the movie scene by the time Lang hired me.

Davidson guided me to a chair and sat across from me on a couch.

"Will you join me in a cocktail?"

"Yes, that would be nice."

She rang for "Too Tall Jones," and again he filled the room.

"Mansfield, we need some drinks. What would you like?"

"Anything's fine."

She directed him to make us a couple of dry martinis.

"Well, Miss Steward, what does T.J. Lang's assistant want with li'l ol' me?"

"Oh, you know who I am?"

"Yes, my secretary filled me in after you called. Plus, I saw you at the funeral and asked someone who you were."

"I'll get right to the point. It's about Lucinda. Do you remember her?"

"Yes, about forty years ago T.J. discovered her in France and brought her back to Hollywood. She made a big splash—several pictures in a row—and won an Oscar for something or other."

"*Remember Daybreak*," I added.

"Yes, that was the picture. Speaking of remember, I also remember that she pushed me into early retirement. But, I guess I should thank her for that.

"Not too long after she caught fire, I met my husband, Fred. To make a long story short, it was the greatest thing that ever happened to me. We have three wonderful kids, six grandchildren, and some great-grandkids on the way."

We talked of many things that afternoon, of the old days and the present. Liz, of course, wanted to know why I was asking her about Lucinda and managed to concoct an idea that I had a possible screenplay about Lang's early career.

After our cordial conversation, I knew Liz Davidson was not the blackmailer. She had left the business herself and, as I looked around, she'd married very well. The blackmailer had to be someone who benefited from Lucinda's sudden departure.

Then the bulb went on. Joan Palmer's career had begun soaring right around the time Lucinda moved to France. Palmer's next movie was great box office and won a best actress Oscar for her.

T.J. produced that one, too. Although there was no way to say for sure, that part probably would have been Lucinda's had she stayed.

I felt that I had my blackmailer, but how was I going to prove it?

Even if she confessed to the outrage, this legendary star of stage, film, and TV could survive any negative press. Come to think of it, the press might come after me—for blowing the whistle on their beloved icon. But then, if I kept everything quiet and the press never got wind of my investigation, no one would be hurt.

I remembered what T.J. said about the two women and the price they paid for their actions. In retrospect, Lucinda won more than she lost. Love is so hard to find. And the love Lucinda still shares with her Lilly has stood the test of time.

On the other hand, all Joan Palmer could show for her life was the public's adulation. That could not have kept her warm on cold nights.

I called Palmer's people and set up a meeting at her Malibu home. I was advised that the location was requested by Ms. Palmer and no one else would be present.

I knew Palmer didn't work that much anymore, but naturally she'd still want to protect her image. Being alone with me (without her publicist) would certainly leave her open and exposed.

I arrived on time and was met at the door by Palmer herself. The years had been very kind to this legend of show business.

"Please come in, Ms. Steward. I've set things up in the living room. I hope tea is all right. I live a very healthy life, and I find tea to be a dignified beverage."

She served the tea and some scones with all the formality and fuss of a fine lady—a role she had played many times.

"What can I do for you, Ms. Steward?"

"I don't know if you know who I am. Your people never questioned me about why I wanted a meeting with you."

"I know. I had anticipated this meeting so I told them you'd be calling."

"I'm sorry, I don't understand. How could you know I'd be calling you?"

"After your meeting with Liz Davidson, she phoned and said you had paid her a visit. I put two and two together. She told me who you were. I guessed I'd be the next one on your list."

"Then you must know why I'm here?"

"Yes, I do. And to answer the question you didn't ask Liz and haven't yet asked me, I'm the person who wrote the note to Lucinda."

21

I was shocked that she just blurted it out that way. I guess she could see it in my face.

"That's why this meeting had to be between us," she continued. "It's not that I worry about the public finding out how I managed my climb in show business. I simply wanted to tell you why I did what I did. And it's not what you think it is. I didn't do it for professional reasons."

I sipped my tea in silence. There would be no need for confrontation and interrogation. Joan was ready to tell all.

"When Lucinda first came to Hollywood, I often saw her around the lot. I even went on her sets a few times to watch her work."

She hesitated momentarily, then took a deep breath, cleared her throat and plunged forward.

"I found myself falling in love with her. And, since she never had a man around, I felt my chances of her returning my affections were good.

"One day, while climbing the back stairwell at Metro, I met her coming down. We were alone and I saw my chance. Our eyes met—she looking down at me, me looking up at her.

"Her stare froze me in my tracks. I couldn't breathe, let alone talk. As she passed I turned and started to say something. 'No, thank you,' she said. 'I already have someone.' I had never been rejected in my life. But Lucinda did, and I hadn't even asked.

"Before Lucinda, I had many offers from ladies around town, but never took them up on their fantasies.

"I never recovered from Lucinda's rejection. And when Lilly came to Hollywood to be with Lucinda, that was more than I could bear. Every night I'd think of Lucinda and Lilly being in love—a love I had convinced myself was mine, and not Lilly's.

"I had them followed to Mexico, and later sent them a letter and photos to blackmail them into leaving.

"Believe me, the last thing I thought about was my career. For the first time in my life, I'd fallen in love.

"I would have given up everything for Lucinda's love. Lilly is a very lucky lady. I understand they're still together."

"Yes, they live in Paris. As a matter of fact, I'll be flying over to see them. Probably next week. T.J. asked me to find out who blackmailed Lucinda and then meet with her and give her the information."

Palmer sat silent for a minute and then made a most surprising suggestion.

22

"Would you mind if I were to tell her myself? Of course, you should be there, too. We can fly over together. Is this all right with you?"

How could I say no?

I finally figured out why T.J. had me do this last job. I figured that he knew who it was all the time. He just wanted me to play the middleman. I was someone who was never involved. I could mediate with all parties.

In the end, it was impossible for me not to feel anything for these two women who did not conform to the images society had created for them. Yet, my feelings were mixed.

I admired Lucinda for choosing love over fame. And I felt sorry for Palmer's lost love and her very lonely life. She had to get her love from her public. In this business, that's a very insecure love.

* * * * *

We didn't talk much on the plane, just small talk. But once we got to our hotel and settled in, Joan felt she needed to tell me how nervous she was, and asked my advice on how she should go about telling Lucinda about her dirty deed.

"Well, if I were you, I'd just tell her straight out, like you told me. Your showing up on her doorstep after all these years should tell her it was you. She must have suspected it was you, anyhow. Have you ever tried to write her? Have you kept in touch over the years?"

"No, I haven't. I guess I was too much of a coward. I was also afraid to communicate with someone I loved very much. I still love her, to this day.

"I guess it would have caused too much pain. Even after forty years, I still have butterflies at the thought of seeing Lucinda."

"Do you want to change your mind? I can go alone to their house and take care of this matter."

"No, I've come this far and I'm not chickening out now. But please stay close."

Then she added, "I know you'd never consider me your friend, but I feel like I've known you my whole life. I can see why T.J. was attracted to you and why he hired you. You have a certain calm about you. T.J. must have needed that calm on more than one occasion."

I had forgotten that she had worked with T.J. on at least five pictures.

23

"My calm comes from living other peoples' lives," I mumbled. "Unfortunately, this job kept me from living my own life."

"There's not much of my life left to offer you," Joan replied, "but I would love to share the remaining time with you."

I didn't know how to answer her. She caught me off guard, and that's a hard thing to do.

"Let's take one thing at a time," I said. "I'll call Lucinda tomorrow and set up a meeting."

Joan had trouble sleeping that night. I could hear her pacing the floor. Then it was quiet. A few minutes later, I heard her crying. I got up and went to her room.

"Ms. Palmer, are you okay? Can I come in?"

"Please do."

"I heard you crying and wanted to know if I could help."

"I guess it's finally hit me—how much damage my jealous deed caused."

"Don't be so hard on yourself. I think Lucinda would have left anyway. She and Lilly were probably getting tired of hiding their relationship."

I sat at the end of Joan's bed and talked her to sleep. When she finally drifted off, I went back to my room.

Morning came. I called Lucinda to set up the meeting. To my amazement, Lucinda informed me she was expecting my visit.

"I'm bringing someone with me," I said, hoping to prepare her to see Palmer.

"That's fine," she replied, apparently unconcerned. We set the time.

I called room service for breakfast and went into Joan's room to wake her up.

"Ms. Palmer, it's time for breakfast. Let's get up. We have a long day ahead of us."

She opened her eyes and fixed them on me. "You were a dear to come into my room last night. I'll never forget your kindness."

Suddenly she realized what day it was.

"Did you call yet? Do we have a meeting?"

"Yes, I called early this morning. Everything is set for noon."

Half smiling, she said, "You mean 'High Noon,' don't you?" We both laughed in the only relaxed moment we had shared up to this point.

At 11 AM, our doorman called up to the room to inform us that our taxi was waiting.

About twenty minutes later we were at Lucinda and Lilly's doorstep. I looked at Joan, winked, and rang the bell. Moments later, a beautiful woman appeared in the doorway.

"Hello, I'm Lilly. And you must be Mary Steward."

"Yes, I am. And this is Joan Palmer."

Joan extended her hand and Lilly took it in hers. We followed her in. There, in the middle of the room, sat Lucinda. She rose to meet us. She caught sight of Joan first.

"It's been too long, old friend. But now you're here, and that's what counts."

Lucinda never laid eyes on me. The next thing I knew, Lilly was beside me.

"Would you like a tour of the house?" I got the message. Those two needed to be alone. Whatever would be said had to be between them, and them alone.

After about an hour of touring the house and grounds and time-filling conversation, Lilly suddenly appeared to receive a subliminal message from Lucinda.

"I think we can return to the living room," she said.

Upon returning, I could sense that everything was settled. "I'm sorry I was not a very good hostess to you when you arrived," Lucinda said to me. "Please forgive me."

"That's all right. I certainly understand."

"Will you join me in my office?"

We left Lilly and Joan.

Lucinda pulled an envelope from her desk drawer.

"T.J. wrote me about what your last task would be. In his letter, he told me to sign a statement verifying you had found my blackmailer."

"But, I got the impression T.J. knew all along that it was Palmer. I also think you also knew who it was."

"You might be right. But think about it. Would Joan have ever talked to T.J., or me? I don't think so. It would have been impossible without you. You are a kind person, like my Lilly. Only you could have brought us all together."

I took the letter and we returned to Lilly and Joan.

"Well, I guess it's time to go," Joan said. "Good-bye, my friends, and take care."

We left knowing this would be our only visit. We returned to California and went our separate ways.

I went to Brad Casey's office to deliver the letter from Lucinda and the million-dollar check I never needed to cash.

"How was your trip?" he asked.

"It was okay. My job is finally over, I hope."

Brad opened the letter and read it.

"Everything looks in order. Here, now read this." He handed me what looked like a will.

"It says that I am T.J.'s sole heir!" I gasped.

"The one and only," Casey confirmed.

Being T.J.'s executor, I knew I'd just inherited an estate in excess of $150 million.

"This is a hell of a Christmas bonus! Thanks, T.J. And the girls thank you, too.

I hope someone with greater resources than I can look into this story and find out which woman actually blackmailed Greta Garbo. Then, maybe people will come forward with the full story, and Garbo can rest in peace. Joan Crawford, in my opinion, will never rest in peace, for her life destroyed so many others.

There's another chapter from Mr. G's past that I believe wholeheartedly: it seems that during World War II, he was a spy for the United States. Again, with no official corroboration, I choose to offer this story through a fictional piece I wrote, called "The Leading Man."

The Leading Man

In 1936 transplanted British actor Andrew Lane was the toast of Hollywood, the kind of actor who could go from dramatic roles to comedy without losing his matinee idol status. One evening, his long-time agent, Sol, called to tell Andrew about a part he simply could not turn down.

After telling Sol to send the script over, Andrew called Washington. The next few months would change the life of one of the most popular screen images of this century, and maybe the course of World War Two.

"Hello. This is Archie Kent. I'm calling to find out about my brother, who is stationed in France."

"Yes, Mr. Kent, we have that information about your brother."

Andrew used code when he called the Naval Intelligence Office at the Pentagon. His agent had told him that the new movie would be shooting in France, and this was the way he told Washington where he was going. This would also give Washington a chance to get their people in place. By the time the cast and crew arrived, the gathering of important information could begin.

The war was just being born in Germany, but most insiders knew that it was only a matter of time before Hitler's armies marched through the capitols of Europe. It was brave men like Andrew Lane who risked their lives trying to keep the rest of the world informed about Hitler.

After reading the script, Andrew called his agent with the okay. The movie would begin shooting in a few days. It was a comedy co-starring a dear friend, Kate Moore.

The script was about an English naval officer falling in love with an American nurse while stationed in Paris. The hook was that the English Naval officer had to dress in drag to get into the States.

Since the macho film star had no problem with his sexuality, the role was easy. His role as a spy would not be so easy. He was told that he would have to contact spies planted in France.

Andrew's social skills would be his most powerful weapons. His charm would be his most useful tool for finding certain lady spies. Before leaving the U.S., Andrew had a meeting with NI agents who briefed him about France.

With codes memorized, Andrew was ready to serve his new-found country. No one in the cast or crew knew what Andrew was up to. They would see him going to parties and spending a lot of his time with the locals, but they expected this of him.

Since he had an international following, it was not hard for him to move in any circle, go to any party, or make friends with people from all walks of life. He was an actor—acting 24 hours a day—always on, and never taking a curtain. This was life for Andrew. He never wanted to stop and simply be who he really was—a very lonely man looking for a love that would never be, a love he never knew as a child.

His mother had left home, taking his love with her. She gave her love to a stranger instead of her husband, a fact that Andrew could never understand. Over the years, he saw his father's pain and could not accept his mother's lack of caring.

Loving anyone became impossible for Andrew. So, for him it was easy to play at love, because his heart was frozen in time, back to the day his mother left.

The time on the ship went by rapidly. The cast and crew spent most of their time trying to learn French. Andrew and Kate took the time to study their lines. At lunch one day, Andrew turned to politics.

"Kate, have you ever thought about what would happen if the world went to war again?"

"No, darling, I just worry about my next movie. War is just a thing men do when one wants more toys than the other. I mean, really, sweets. War is for real people, we actor types don't qualify."

Kate was on a roll. "Remember, our guns fire blanks. After the director yells 'Cut,' the dead guys get up and go home. What's all this stuff about war? Have you been reading the paper again? That's dangerous, dear, and it could be habit forming."

"No, I haven't been reading the paper," Andrew replied, deciding that he had better drop the subject. Kate knew him too well, and he didn't want to sound too serious.

"Now, Katie, you know the only part of the paper I read is Hedda's column. All those lies she writes about us keeps everyone guessing. Of course, if I ever take the plunge, you'll be the first to know."

The ship approached the coast of France and the movie company readied their equipment for unloading. Andrew and Kate went to their hotel and began looking for the best place for dinner and dancing.

It was important to be seen in the right places and be with the right people. It was all part of the business. Andrew phoned Kate.

"Darling, ready for drinks and dinner? I hear that you eat late and dance 'till dawn."

"Pet, just lead me to the bar," Kate replied. "Dinner will take care of itself."

As the world famous movie lovers swept into the room looking like they just left make-up and wardrobe, all eyes were fixed on the glamorous duo. The manager stepped forward and seated the new arrivals himself.

"Good evening, dear friends. Welcome to my little café. Paris has been waiting for the two of you with arms opened."

With that, the manager placed his arms around Kate and acted like a long-lost cousin. "Please let me serve you tonight. I will not take no for an answer."

"My dear friend, we are yours to command." Andrew replied. "Bring on your best. We are in your hands."

As this act was playing out, in the corner of the bar a woman was watching every move Andrew made. Though long used to admiring glances, her presence and beauty were not lost on the actor.

Food was on the table in minutes, and the couple reveled in the selections the manager had made for them. After dinner, the manager advised that the entertainment would soon begin, and they moved to the bar. Andrew didn't waste time finding his admirer.

He looked her way and raised his glass in a toast. She answered with her glass, and a smile. He sent the waiter over with a note inviting her to join their table.

Andrew immediately sensed that this woman was not the everyday fan. Tall, stately and stunning, she walked like an actress but glowed like a countess. He rose to greet her.

"My dear, Andrew Lane is my name."

"Yes, Mr. Lane, we very much enjoy your pictures here in Paris. Many of our young women are madly in love with you."

"And you?" Andrew asked so impishly.

She smiled, her steel-blue eyes burning into his. Andrew changed the subject.

"Paris does not do their women justice. Tell me your name so I can burn the letters into my heart."

"My name is Lara."

"Lara what?" Andrew asked.

"Lara is enough for now. Last names are so silly for women. When a man takes a woman to marry, he just takes her name away anyway."

Katie offered, "She's got you there, pal. Sit down, my dear. You are what we call in the States 'a real dame.' Lara, I'm Kate Moore."

"Yes, I'm very fond of your work."

"By the way, love," Kate countered before Lara could say anything more, "don't ever get into the picture business. I have enough trouble with Davis and Garbo without a knockout like you running around the lot."

"Don't worry, I can't act."

Kate laughed. "Neither can I, honey, but don't tell Davis and Garbo."

"Would you care to join us for the entertainment?" Andrew asked.

"Thank you, but no. I have to meet a friend and I am already late." Then, pausing and reflecting as a good actress would, she added, "I hope to be here again tomorrow night."

"Well then, good night, my dear." Andrew kissed her hand. He would dream of her and her soft manner that night—a manner that spoke of someone who knew of life and love.

Many people say the French are ruled by love and its passion. That was something Andrew could only dream about. Love was just a word that had no meaning; it was just a sound without feeling.

Until this evening, Andrew could only guess at love. Now, suddenly, he had found someone who might open a door. He fought the feeling. Lara is not real, he said to himself. She is a temporary illusion of everything wonderful. She can only live in a man's dream.

* * * * *

Getting the movie started and gathering information was the task at hand. He would begin by cruising the nightspots looking for people who knew the truth about France—people who knew when and where Hitler would strike. Naval Intelligence had briefed Andrew that there were agents already planted in Paris, advance people who could direct the German army to the easy targets. These were people who would betray their home, their families and their country for the new world order of fascism. Andrew's mission was an important part of the silent effort to ensure that France and Paris should not fall.

It was a long night, and Andrew came up empty. No one seemed to know much about anything. Paris was alive with life. War was not given the time of day. "How sad," Andrew thought, "that Hitler might just walk into Paris without firing a shot."

The next night was about the same as the first. Andrew and Kate made their entrance and ate in peace. The bar entertainment was great, but they cut the evening short because there was an early call for the first day of shooting.

The first scene was in a field. Andrew was supposed to drive a motorcycle into a haystack. The scene took forever to get right. At the lunch break, Andrew was surprised to see Lara on the set and coming his way.

"So this is how they make movies," she said cheerily, as if chatting with him on a movie set was an everyday occurrence. "What a truly hard life you lead."

"It beats working for a living. Say, what brings you here?"

"I live in the village that your company will be using in the film."

This Lara was a much different person than the Lara he met the night before in the restaurant. She was more natural, more real. She seemed less ethereal, more outdoorsy. Her blue eyes shined in the sunlight. Her golden hair danced around her face as she spoke. Andrew wished he could stop time so that he could stare at her longer and bask in her radiance.

31

"We are going to be done in an hour or so. Would you like to take me on a grand tour of your beautiful countryside?"

"I would like that very much."

"Wait over there." Andrew pointed to a group of chairs where extras hung out between takes. "I'll be with you soon."

Andrew then walked over to Kate's dressing area. "Katie, after I finish with that haystack, I'm going to explore France with Lara."

"Look, buddy, don't get in over your head. This girl might be too much for a little guy from Bristol."

"Thanks for thinking of me, kid, but I guess it's about time I tried the waters."

* * * * *

Andrew and Lara talked as they walked. First, Andrew told Lara of himself and his life before Hollywood. He told her of his home in England. He told her of a motherless childhood, a subject that he had never talked about before. She in turn talked about a childhood spent in boarding schools and of parents she never really knew.

In many ways, their backgrounds were so similar that it was almost frightening. Their lives had so paralleled that they could finish each other's thoughts. This was suddenly going too fast for Andrew. Love was not supposed to be part of this assignment.

For the next few days, Lara and Andrew were joined at the hip. One night, Kate came to Andrew's room to talk.

"Dear friend, what is going on with you and your Paris princess?"

"I really don't know. For the first time in my life I feel part of someone, or something, besides myself. I feel that I don't have to be Andrew Lane. I can just be myself, Archie Kent. In our business, people like Lara are hard to find. I think, old girl, I just might have caught one of Cupid's arrows."

"Great stuff, you old bugger. Maybe she'll fill that hole in the middle of your chest."

Andrew smiled. "I can always count on you to put in your two cents. I haven't gone down the aisle yet, so don't go playing the wedding march. I think I must go a lot slower though, so as not to scare off the poor girl."

"If you have a plan, count me in. I should love helping you sweep this girl off her feet. After all, if I remember right, you were the one who introduced me to my now ex-fifth husband."

"Sorry, old girl. Maybe there is a Frenchman around here with your name on him."

After dinner, Lara and Andrew went out on the town. He had intelligence to gather. He hated using Lara, but she did know Paris and all of the people who were coming and going. She might be helpful finding out about the local big wigs.

"Darling," Andrew asked, "do you know much of what goes on around here?"

"Why do you ask me this? Is it important?"

"I was just wondering about where I might want to settle down."

Andrew felt he was pushing too hard, but hoped Lara bought his story. The subject was closed.

A few days later, Lara, surprisingly, brought up the subject of America. "Someday I would like to see America. They say it will be the future of the world. Do you believe this, dear?"

Andrew was stunned. He could not believe his ears. While training as a spy he remembered learning how to spot a spy. Lara was showing all of the signs. Asking questions about the U.S. and its leadership role in the world was a dead giveaway.

If Andrew could have crawled in a hole and pulled it closed behind him, he would have. His Lara was undoubtedly a spy—someone he was sent to get information from, not give information to.

How ironic! His heart ached for love and affection, but Andrew knew what he must do. He had to string Lara along and try to get as much information as he could.

As much as he wanted to tell Kate about Lara, he could not. Doing so would reveal his other life and possibly put Kate in danger. Carrying on would be difficult, but not impossible.

As time grew short, Andrew knew getting information from Lara was his only avenue. She was also falling in love and might feel as vulnerable as he certainly did.

Calling upon all of his acting skills, Andrew slowly began to draw out the vital information he needed. But, was he really that clever, or was Lara choosing to cooperate?

* * * * *

As Andrew got the information out to America, the Nazis learned—much too late—that Lara was their leak. Someone was dispatched from Germany to assassinate her. They were also hoping to get the American agent at the same time.

It was the last night before the cast and crew left for the States. By this time Kate knew the fire that was in Andrew's and Lara's love was all but out, but she could not know the real reason.

Maybe in another time or place these two could have been one. Andrew never really had a cause—only a debt owed to his new country. Lara, on the other hand, did have a cause.

It would be a cause she would die for. Hitler had a way of making the people of Germany see a future that would never be.

Andrew asked Lara to take one last walk down the road where they had fallen in love.

"No, dearest," she told him. "I must walk down this road alone. Do not leave the hotel tonight. Please. You must give me your word."

"Okay, but promise me that you will go straight home. No picking up strange men along the way."

The book on spying says, "better them than me."

I always wondered why, during the McCarthy hearings, that Mr. G was never called. Now I know why. I don't think anyone in their right mind would ever challenge Mr. G's love of America. I sometimes feel bad that I am not a better writer because I don't feel I'm doing justice to these memorable stories.

Once, after giving a party for the old crowd, I asked him if the stories I had just heard were true.

"Mary, you must understand that we are actors, and paid to tell stories. Some of us don't know where the story ends and the truth begins."

"And, of course, Mr. G, you always knew the difference."

"Yes, that is true," he replied. "I always tell the truth."

For every person who betrayed Mr. G, there were ten who didn't. The very elegant Deborah Kerr was one of those people. He used to say that she knew more about him than he knew about himself. Their movie *An Affair To Remember* was one of Mr. G's favorites. He said that making that film was not work, more like being with friends at a party. If you ever wondered why women still cry at the movie's closing scene, it's because Mr. G was not playing Deborah's lover, but in fact, was playing her friend. Women sense when a man cares, and Mr. G was that kind of man. He could make love to you with only a kiss, or maybe he would just hold you in his arms, and you could feel the warmth and comfort that only a friend could give.

The sharp-tongued, feisty Katherine Hepburn was another member of the Grant group of the '30s and '40s. Mr. G told me that she had a problem with the real world and could only live her life through her movie roles. He said that she had a fantasy about Spencer Tracy. Mr. G tried to arrange a marriage between Hepburn and Howard Hughes, but she backed out, preferring to live in a make-believe world of Tracy-Hepburn. Mr. G said that he didn't think their union would hear the pitter-patter of little feet. And I guess lifetime friendship suited them both well. A strong man like Howard Hughes scared Hepburn to death, so Mr. G gave up on his friend ever getting married

Speaking of Howard Hughes, Mr. G recalled one favorite story about the time he and Hughes put a posse together after a rancher left his barn door open and his cows got loose. He said they referred to it as the "Great Palm Springs Round-Up." What made the story so funny was that the posse consisted of Hughes, Mr. G, David Niven, Gary Cooper, John Wayne and Errol Flynn. Mr. G said that he and Cooper rounded up some horses and began going from house to house asking if they could go into backyards in search of wayward cows. The posse was pressed into service by a sheriff who was attending a party at Hughes' Palm Springs home. To say that our cowboys were two sheets to the wind is an understatement.

Picture this. It's 2 A.M. and you hear a knock at your door. As you open the door, peering through your sleepy eyes, there stand Howard Hughes, Cary Grant, David Niven, and Gary Cooper. After the shock wears off, you realize you have four drunken cowboys on your porch and the only thing you can say is, "Sure, go in my backyard and round up all the cows you want, but don't wake me up again."

On another visit to the Springs, Mr. G said that he and Hughes came up with the perfect invention. It seems Hughes was sure Los Angeles would grow too big with too many cars, and there would be smog. Now remember, this was in the late '40s when Hughes figured this all out. So, he said that they should build giant fans to keep the smog out of their beloved Palm Springs. The next time you pass through the valley into Palm Springs, look up into the hills and tell me what you see. There must be at least 2,000 giant fans dotting the hills in and around the road to Palm Springs. Mr. G used to say Hughes was a little crazy, but never dumb.

And then there was the beautiful Ingrid Bergman. Mr. G said she was well read and a wonderful person to be around. In the end, she had put all of the pieces of her life back together, but her early life was not such an easy puzzle.

She loved her craft, worked hard at it. She was a real pro. She never understood why her private life was so important to the American press. When she publicly said she was having an affair outside of her marriage, it was the end of her career. Mr. G's philosophy was that actors were actors 24 hours a day, and those actors who think otherwise will lose their public, and maybe even their lives.

If you are a strong person and do not take your career seriously, you will survive. If you believe you owe the public nothing and think you are that person up on the screen, you will be in trouble. Maybe that's why the drug business is doing so well in Hollywood.

In Mr. G's era, the actors would have these fantasy parties in the Hollywood Hills. They'd come in and change into their make-believe world. The men would dress in expensive frocks, wrapped in feathers and silk, and the women swaggered around smoking cigars in their tuxedos, and this would be more than enough to fulfill their sexual appetites. God forbid they would live the same lives as the people who paid to see their movies.

Earlier, I said I would talk about the gay side of Hollywood. In one of my side trips and life experiences, I played Judy Garland at La Cage Aux Folles. Popular male stars were dating our cast members on any given night. This was a shock to me at first, but later, after I saw so many of them slip in and out our back door sweeping my friends off their feet, it became commonplace. The reason I chose not to out them is because they have accepted the image the public wants, and they act accordingly.

When I told Mr. G that I had escaped becoming Mrs. Fred Astaire (later, I found out Fred was giving a well known young, male star midnight dance lessons), he laughed and said that he could go back and pick out certain actors in Hollywood who needed to be married in his day, and there would be little difference from the actors of today. For instance Danny Kaye would be any one of the comedy superstars who grace the silver screen today. Rock Hudson could be represented today by the handsome leading men who have joined cults to hide behind their lavender walls.

Now, the mystique of Garbo would be the enigma of a Jodie Foster. Only, Garbo gave up Hollywood for her private life. Fortunately, I believe Jodie Foster in present day Hollywood can live her life.

Now, on the other side of the coin we have the very brave Ellen Degeneres who fought the anti-gay war via the TV airways. Later we noticed that other gay-themed TV shows came after, and by Ellen putting her neck on the block, she took the first hit. I truly believe Disney (ABC) encouraged her and then when things went bad, hid out in Fantasyland until the smoke cleared. Now, I see Ellen is alive and well at CBS. I only hope someday Mickey Mouse plants a big kiss on Ellen (squarely on her ass).

Now that I think of it, Disney has been gay-friendly for a long time. Now, it's so clear why Mickey never married Minnie. He obviously had the hots for Donald Duck. Walt, you little devil! I bet you always wanted to be Snow White but never had the guts to go drag. If Mr. G were alive today he would find this all a big joke. During the Disney Christmas season, Mr. G would do the Christmas readings in the square on Main Street. At that time, it was called the candlelight service, and Mr. G's readings were always super. For his services, Walt Disney would open the doors to his Magic Kingdom so Jennifer and her friends could enjoy the park. Also, a membership to Walt's private Club 33 was a nice touch. Disney was far ahead of his time in PR. I miss his smile and humor. Mr. G counted him as a friend, and was always there if needed.

* * * * *

In 1992, my best friend, Lori Cain, talked me into putting pen to paper. In this book, I lovingly refer to my "various side trips." But in my first attempt at literary immortality, *I Could Have Been Mrs. Fred Astaire,* you will find a life that never stood still—a life that was full of great friends and very dangerous enemies. Thoroughbred racing always highlighted my world, and to this day I look back with great pleasure when remembering those happy times. But don't get me wrong: racing was not all fun and games.

Again, you will read a fictional short story, *Sales Topper,* based on a true story. I have changed all of the names except for one of the characters, Jacque Noe'l, my real-life lover. Jacque died in an auto accident outside Paris. He was returning from California, and the trip was to be a meeting with his parents to announce our engagement.

Thank God for fiction. It helps to keep friends and loved ones alive. When I first wrote *I Could Have Been Mrs. Fred Astaire,* a true story, I had no idea I would be adding it to a book. I hope you enjoy it. After reading *ICHBMFA*, I will cover some things in greater detail.

I Could Have Been Mrs. Fred Astaire

Finding My Place

Being raised on the beach has great benefits—you don't need clothes. But like all kids, I eventually longed for a life other than the one I was living. At the age of twenty this longing became even stronger.

While attending college, I met a girl who had horses at a lay-up center near my house. The first time I saw these big, beautiful animals I knew I would spend my life working with them.

I guess almost everyone has a soft spot for animals. To be part of an animal's life is something so special that it cannot be put into words. Maybe as you read my story you will understand the great respect and love I feel for my four-legged friends.

After my college friend sold her horses and moved away, the owner of the lay-up center offered me a job. I guess the owner had

L-R: Mrs. McCracken, Cedar Post (with author in the saddle), and Mr. Charlie McCracken. This was the poor horse I had to learn on. He was stabled at the ranch where I got my start, and, God bless him, he never bucked me off or bit me. And that was saying a lot . . . with someone on his back who didn't know what end to get up on.

watched me working with my friend's horses and liked what she saw. My duty was to gallop all the horses that were laid up there. These included some two-year-old racehorses, and I became a friend of thoroughbred trainer Henry Moreno.

Mr. Moreno had some horses stabled at the lay-up center and encouraged me to go to Santa Anita, but when I asked him for a job, he said he didn't need any help. He suggested that I could free-lance (work for various trainers). This, I found out, was easier said than done. After a few days, I found myself walking around the barn area more than riding. I was new and had to find one barn I could build a reputation on. Little did I know that the barn I was to start my career in already had its own reputation.

Her name was Daphine Collins. Hearing that name for the first time, I thought I was going to meet some very beautiful English horsewoman who would help me start my career. Hello, Earth to me! Welcome to the real world. Ms. Collins was a short, stocky and mean lady, but one of the finest horsewomen I have ever worked for. After getting over the shock of finding out I was to be nothing more than a slave, I figured out that this was to be my apprenticeship. As I look back, I think that working with this gruff old lady turned out to be the reason I got as far as I did in racing. Not a day goes by without me thinking what a great time it really was.

Ms. Collins knew I wanted to gallop, but said I must learn from the bottom up which translated means work 18 hours a day and eat very little. When I asked Ms. Collins for food (part of our room and board agreement), she made her feelings clear.

"You want to gallop horses, don't you?" she asked.

"Yes I do."

"Well, you must watch your weight."

This, I must add, was the only time Ms. Collins made any reference to my galloping. I look back on her ploy now as one born out of her thriftiness. So, occasionally I stole our poor horses' carrots. In fact, I ate so many carrots I could see the seat numbers in the grandstand from the back side!

After the Del Mar meet, I parted company with my mentor and found a job with trainer Reggie Cornell. I guess a lot of people felt sorry for me during my employment with Ms. Collins. They could see I needed help. Reggie knew I had a good work ethic and was not afraid of much. You see, after ten weeks under Ms. Collins, I found I had developed great courage. Still, Reggie had enough gallop help, so once again I found myself working around the barn and, most important of all, learning. The staff in Reggie's barn went out of their way to help me.

This was Santa Anita with a different style of trainer. I found I had much to learn. I also made a lot of friends in other barns—something I was never allowed to do while I worked in Ms. Collins' barn.

When I felt enough confidence, I went to Reggie and announced, "I'm going to freelance gallop."

"Good luck," he said, "and when you get hungry, your job will still be here."

Little did he know, I'd already been through that part of my career. The next few days were spent galloping for small barns with fewer than five head. If any aspiring exercise rider reads this story, my advice is to take this road. You will find every kind of personality that a horse can exhibit. I could not name all of the horsemen who helped me during my freelance days, but they know who they are. God bless you all!

While freelancing, one always keeps an ear open and hopes a steady barn job opens up (salaried, working for one barn only.) Well, one of the trainers I was freelancing for asked if I wanted to gallop horses for the east coast trainer he was working for. This dream job was with a stately gentleman trainer by the name of Buddy Hirsch, who would be here for the Santa Anita meet.

Once, he referred to me in the *Racing Form* as more "racetrack" than the gallop girls he hired off the farms. Later, I figured out what he meant by that and it served me well throughout my career. Being "racetrack" was my best defense when I had to be tough and fight to survive. Working with Mr. Hirsch also gave me a good understanding of the eastern branch of our business. Mr. Hirsch said that after Santa Anita was over he would be returning to the east coast. He asked me to join him. I was finishing college and told him that I could not leave at that time. I asked if he could recommend me to any other trainers he knew that were based in California. He said he knew a trainer, but didn't know if he would hire a girl. The trainer's name was Charlie Whittingham.

The first morning I showed up, Mr. Whittingham told me to put my walking shoes on. He only had an opening for a hot-walker. Remember now, I had been galloping Grade I horses for Mr. Hirsch, so to say I felt let down is an understatement. Then again, I knew this was a test. I heard Mr. Whittingham was a trainer who demanded 100% of an employee. He also had to know if someone could take anything he threw at them with no questions asked. Well, bring on the empty horses. Then, one day, the following happened, even though it might sound like a movie script.

It was a Monday morning and I had just finished walking my first horse. Ed Lambert, the foreman for the barn, came to me and said one of the boys didn't show up. Did I have my boots and helmet with me? Being the kind of person I was (always positive), I kept my stuff in one of the tack rooms.

"Yes!" I exclaimed.

"Then go get on Bargain Day."

At the time, he was the most wonderful horse I had ever seen. I only hoped that this kind-looking horse wouldn't pull my butt off. That always makes you look bad. I entered the gap with the first set and started jogging Bargain Day off. Then, at about the 7/8 pole I began galloping. The first set went great and so did the next five sets after that. The morning was over, and my tennis shoes were retired.

As I walked to the parking lot, a very nice man by the name of Oscar Otties, a *Racing Form* writer, asked me if I knew I had just

Trainer Burt Litrail, and author. This was during my freelance days (pre Charles Whittingham). As you can see, La Cage Aux Folles was not the first time I had to dress up as a man. In those days, women were not welcome in the backside. But time has shown us that women play a big part in the horse racing game.

made history. I thought he was kidding me. He then explained that I was the first girl to gallop a Whittingham horse on the track. I told him that I was just trying to get a good-paying job.

Mr. Otties and I became good friends over the next few years. He encouraged me to use my education to write and document my life in this wonderful business of racing. Today, one can look in almost any thoroughbred horse racing media guide and see how I

Hall of Fame trainer Charles Whittingham, and author, looking over the day's entries at Santa Anita.

fared as an exercise rider for Mr. Whittingham between 1970 and 1977—the money won, national titles and, of course, the pride. To me, it was always the pride that mattered most since I never saw much of the money.

Losing A Friend

I thought I was prepared for most things that can happen in a barn, good and bad, but nothing can prepare you for the worst thing that can happen—the death of a horse. My first experience with this came on a bright sunny afternoon at Hollywood Park.

We had just gotten Linda's Chief in our barn from Bobby Frankel's. The Chief was not the average Whittingham horse. The day he came to our barn, I knew he would never make it. As a two-year-old, he was run off his legs. By the time he got to us as a three-year-old, he was done. When I passed his stall I could see in his eyes a look that seemed to say, "Oh no, do I have to go to the track

Charlie Whittingham, and author during an early morning workout. Charlie's last words to me before leaving the barn were "hang on kid, we're betting on this one today . . . so for God's sakes, don't fall off, and try and keep him between the fences." Charlie always could make you feel good about your job. Too bad the boss of today can't do that.

today?" I don't think I have ever known a horse that was so human-like. In the back of my mind I knew he felt he would be better off dead than being a racehorse. He was burned out.

Please, for you people who bet your $2.00, remember the worst that can happen is you lose your bet. The worst thing a horse can lose is his life.

Going over to the paddock on race day, I could not shake the feeling that Chief was planning something. He was calm and collected. Knowing this horse like I did, I knew this was not normal.

Hollywood Gold Cup winner Ancient Title, and author. Charlie Whittingham loaned me out to another trainer (Keith Stukie) because "AT" was only galloped by a girl. Keith's daughter ("AT's" regular rider) was hurt in a backside accident, so Keith needed a girl to gallop "AT." Since our barn was across the road from Keith's, Charlie let me gallop "AT" before I started work at our barn. Cutting to the chase: "AT," and the horse I was galloping for Charlie, met in the Hollywood Gold Cup. "AT" won, and Charlie's horse was second. Charlie never loaned me out again.

Author and Hollywood Gold Cup winner Quack on the turf at Santa Anita for an early morning workout.

He was usually wild-eyed and washy. That day, Steve Valdez was his rider. Steve had worked him in the morning, and the Chief really got along with him. I guess that was because Steve, like me, felt sorry for the little guy and did everything he could to make the morning go by faster.

When the horses were in the starting gate and the "flag is up" was announced, I held my breath. It did not take long before my worst fears were confirmed. When the gates opened, the Chief dropped his shoulder, unseating Steve (perhaps unloading him?) Only the Chief and his Maker knew what was about to happen in

World-record-holder Rich Cream (with author aboard) during a morning workout at Hollywood Park racetrack.

the next few seconds. Without going through the painful memory of his last few minutes on Earth, to say he broke every bone in his body when he went over the rail is an understatement.

That day was twice as hard on me because I was in charge of the paddock work (assisting Mr. Whittingham). This made the Chief my responsibility after the accident. As I lay on the cold cement, I looked in his eyes and felt a great calm come over me. Unfortunately, we could not send him to that Big Track in the Sky until after the ninth race. The State Vet had to be there for insurance. From the seventh race to the ninth race, I held the Chief in my arms and told him of the better world he would be going to. Finally, the ninth race was over. The chief's death was quick and painless. If such a thing is possible, then this was the only animal suicide ever recorded. I only wish I was not the one who had to record it.

From an owner or fan's point of view, it could be asked, "Why would Charlie run the Chief?" Well, Charlie Whittingham thought that with light training and some time between races, Linda's Chief might work through. Charlie gave every horse its chance to be good or bad. As far as Bobby Frankel was concerned, if he knew then what he knows now, he might have gone slower.

Multiple-stakes-winning star Quack from the barn of Charlie Whit-
tingham. He liked his picture taken more then I did. As you can see,
Charlie not only taught his horses to run fast . . . but also to smile
for the camera.

God only knows what happened that afternoon at Hollywood
Park. I believe that the Chief met his destiny and no one could have
stopped it.

Marje's Mistake

Another tragedy I witnessed in our barn could have been
avoided. We had just won the Santa Anita Handicap with Stardust
Mel, and were headed for Hollywood Park and the Gold Cup.

The Handicap was run in the mud, and Stardust Mel was
born of Wallet Lifter, who many people thought must have been

foaled in the mud. When Mel got to Hollywood, the track was hard and he was having trouble staying sound. When his owner, Marje Everett, asked me how her horse was going, I told her the truth. I said he would not train well at Hollywood Park. She should lay him up until Del Mar. That way, he'd be okay. At that point, Mrs. Everett switched from horsewoman to racetrack owner.

"I'm having so many complaints about my track I don't dare *not* run. My horse has to run in the Gold Cup—no matter his condition."

Unlike Linda's Chief, we did not lose Mel. But his racing days were over. I learned a new lesson—money talks, and poo-poo walks.

Oh, by the way—Stardust Mel was sold to Sandy Hawley's wife for $1.00, then went on to be a champion jumper in Canada.

The Mismatched Match Race

One morning, Charlie announced that our filly, Miss Musket, was to run in a match race.

"Who's the other horse?" I asked.

"The eastern filly, Chris Evert."

"Any relation to Marje?"

"Only in money won."

Charlie and I always tried to top each other when it came to jokes.

The match was scheduled for the end of the Hollywood Park meet. Since I was already at Del Mar, I had to drive up for the press conference. Pat Rogerson of the *Racing Form* was the host, and I represented the Whittingham stable.

Before the press conference I had breakfast with the Joneses (Aaron and Marie), the owners of Miss Musket. The one lesson Charlie taught me was that when an owner asked about a horse I galloped, I was to tell the truth. So, after we ate, Aaron asked me if I thought we could beat Chris Evert. For the last few days, Miss Musket had not been training well, and I think Charlie felt she was not going to do her best. I knew he wanted to scratch her. Later Charlie told me Marje talked him out of it. If I know Marje, she probably told Charlie that the future of Hollywood Park and racing was in his hands. You see, Charlie took his role of leading trainer very seriously.

He was always protective of the sport's image. Marje probably also told Charlie how much the fans would be disappointed if Miss Musket did not run. This would have devastated Charlie. The only thing Charlie loved more than his horses was the racing fan. He always held a great deal of respect for the $2 bettor. I must agree. If it was not for the $2 bettor, Charlie might be pumping gas and I would have won a Tony or an Oscar by now.

I told Aaron and Marie that I didn't think we could win. (I heard a rumor later that Aaron called his insurance company and insured his bet, which was winner-take-all for $350,000!) After breakfast, Aaron, Marie and I went to the *Daily Racing Form* press conference. It was quite something to see.

There were at least 500 people there. It was one of the most exciting shows any racetrack has ever put on. (Too bad the race couldn't live up to the media hype.) Pat let the Chris Evert people go first. They backed up their egotistical opinion of themselves with the exploits of their really great filly. One by one, they informed the crowd how and why they should win. Then the room was quiet. Since I was a regular on Pat's weekly handicapping show, most of the crowd knew me. I knew if I was not truthful, they would know it.

I opened with a welcome to our east coast visitors. I then made it short and not so sweet. "They will break out of the gate at the quarter-pole gap. One horse will try to make the gap, and the other one will win by 31 lengths."

You could have heard a pin drop. I looked at Aaron and Marie, and they smiled. Because I had told them my thoughts earlier, they were not surprised. They were the only ones in the building who knew what was coming. Pat jumped to his feet. He was completely caught off guard. As a rule, he could always count on me for at least twenty minutes. After the crowd buzz had quieted, Pat had only one question, and he said it as slow as humanly possible.

"But, who makes the gap, and who wins by 31 lengths?"

"For the price of admission, you'll find out."

I bet Marje loved that. There were too many people's feelings to consider to say any more.

The flag went up. The horses broke. Miss Musket tried to make the gap and, Chris Evert won by 30. I missed by one length, but I still had Charlie's respect, and Aaron and Marie to this day are still great friends.

I must add that great horses can't be great 24 hours a day, seven days a week. In defense of Miss Musket and because of barn pride, I have to say she had her moments. Maybe it was PMS that day (Pre-Match Sulkiness), and she just didn't fire. She never had to prove herself to us, because we loved her. If you want to keep score,

(Tarzan of the '50s Jock Mahony (and also Sally Fields' stepfather) and author sharing a moment at the poolside of "Winners Circle Lodge" at Del Mar, California.

East vs. West, suffice to say that we sent plenty of our eastern friends home broke.

Racing Goes Hollywood

As long as there is racing, there will be movie stars going to the races. They have owned and bred their own horses dating back to the Bing Crosby-Del Mar days. The list of celebrities in our barn were a mix of today and yesterday.

The first owner that I met was Greer Fogelson (Greer Garson), owner of Forked Lightning Ranch and 1971 Horse of the Year Ack Ack. She turned out to be more horsewoman than movie star. Her husband Buddy was a true gentleman breeder. They both were very gracious and remained my friends for years.

The next celebs that come to mind were Angie Dickinson and Burt Bacharach. They had a little girl named Nikki, and at the Del Mar meet I sometimes took care of her. Burt and Angie were a different breed of owner—more movie stars than horsemen. It seemed it was more of a distraction for them than a real passion. Nonetheless,

L-R: Santa Anita Handicap winner and winner of the Hollywood Gold Cup, Ack Ack, with groom Eugene, and author, going over to the paddock, Gold Cup Day at Hollywood Park. "Ack" was a Horse of the Year and owned by Greer Garson Folgenson (long-winded Oscar-winning actress).

Burt still enjoys the sport. In later years, I found myself closer to Angie than Burt. She has come to my aid with her support for my script (*Garbo's Secret*), and encourages me to keep my focus and hang in there. In this town, that kind of friendship is very rare. But Angie, you must understand, is the rarest jewel of them all.

Then there is Jack Klugman, star of stage, screen and television. I really believe Jack acts to support his racing. I became friends with Jack when I went through the clubhouse recruiting celebs for a bowling tournament that was to be an HBPA fundraiser. Even since that tournament, Jack and I would talk racing when I visited his sets (*Odd Couple* and *Quincy*.) Unlike most of the celebs, the gods of racing smiled down on Jack by way of his beloved Jaklin Klugman.

From the first day that horse stepped on the racetrack, Jack knew that racing would take over his life. It was great to see Jack happy and making money, and not losing money at the betting windows. As of this writing, Jaklin Klugman is ranked number six in California for prodigy earnings, and is producing winners.

*L-R: Hall of Fame Jockey Bill Shoemaker, the author, Nikkii Bachar-
ach, and Emmy-winning and Oscar-nominated Angie Dickenson at
a Del Mar Racetrack fundraiser basketball game. Burt's team won,
and of course I was on Burt's team. After Burt and Angie broke up,
I stayed friends with both, for Nikkii's sake. In the end, even though
they have gone their separate ways, they will always share a heart
. . . Nikkii's*

The next celebrity I came in contact with changed my life.
Charlie had sent me to Del Mar early with some horses during Hollywood Park. I had finished my morning's work and was back in my
room. The phone rang and I thought it was my boyfriend, David.

"Please hold for Cary Grant," the voice on the other end of
the line said.

"David, quit playing games. I'm tired and I'm going to take
a nap." I hung up. A few minutes later, the phone rang again. I
thought it was David and hung up a second time. Finally, I went off
to sleep, planning my revenge for his joke.

Two hours later, the phone rang again. This time it was the
front desk. A very excited desk lady said, "Mary, you will not believe
me when I tell you who was just here asking for your room number!"

"Who's that?"

L-R: The author, Charles Whittingham (above pro bowler Don Carter), Bill Shoemaker, Angie Dickenson, and Burt Bacharach.

"Cary Grant," she replied, trembling, "and he acts like he's mad!"

In that one terrible moment I realized that the early calls were not David's, but I tried to convince myself that the desk lady was part of the joke. I didn't have to wait long to find out the truth. There was a quiet knock at the door. As I walked to the door I thought, "What in the hell would Cary Grant need or want from me?"

When I opened the door, fear must have shown in my eyes, but when our eyes met, instead of being angry at my hang-ups he smiled and said, "As you can see, I *am* Cary Grant." I didn't know what to say. "May I come in please?"

I couldn't speak. I moved from the doorway to let him pass. He sat on the couch and could see I had not a clue as to why he was there. He started to explain why our lives had come together at this time.

"First, Mary, has Charlie told you of my conversation with Mrs. Everett?"

L-R: Oscar-winning composer Burt Bacharach, Cary Grant, and the author at an award ceremony honoring the author as HBPA "Woman of the Year" for her fundraising efforts.

L-R: (top row) Emmy-award actor Jack Klugman, Angie Dickenson, Bill Shoemaker, Burt Bacharach, and Hall of Fame Jockey Laffit Pincay, Jr., and (bottom row) the author, during a PBA Celebrity Bowling tournament. Shoe and I teamed up and beat the pants off everyone.

"No, I'm not aware of any conversation you had with Charlie or Mrs. Everett."

"Well, I asked Mrs. Everett if she knew anyone I could hire to teach my daughter to ride."

"No, I didn't know that."

"Charlie and Mrs. Everett both think you would be a great teacher for Jennifer. Would you like to work for me?" Before I could think of what to say, the Cary Grant charm had already worked its magic.

"Sure, of course. Bring her down anytime. I'll be happy to help."

If it were anyone else, I would have asked when, where and how much! But this was Cary Grant. I trusted he was just like in his movies and could be taken at his word. The following weekend, the Grants, Cary and Jennifer, were at the barn ready for Jennifer's first lesson. For the next few years, Cary Grant was just Jennifer's Daddy

L-R: Cary Grant, author, Bill Shoemaker, and Burt Bacharach. As you can see, Mr G is looking down at my bum. What Burt could not see, but Mr G could, was that Shoe had his hand down the back of my dress. Shoe knew I didn't wear undies so he had a hand full of MARY. Mr G could see everything, and was amazed that I never turned a hair.

to me. As time went on, I knew Mr. G appreciated me for treating him like that.

Occasionally, this was hard to do because of his celebrity status. On any given day or night, Mr. G's guests could include Princess Grace, Larry Olivier, Kate or Audrey Hepburn, Ingrid Bergman, Nat and R.J. Wagner, Greta Garbo, and kings and queens of industry—plus a very strange visitor by the name of Howard Hughes. It was quite a culture shock for a 20-year-old kid from Long Beach!

Remember, though, that I was only the hired help and not privileged to their friendship. But I sure heard some great stories. Later, I would ask Mr. Grant if the stories were true. He would only say, "We are paid to tell stories as actors and some of us don't know when to quit acting."

Some stories took some explaining, and Mr. G was great at correcting his friends' tales. But, that's another book.

As Jennifer got older, the horses were slowly giving way to school and college. Even though I no longer worked for Mr. G after Jennifer went away to school, he always was a friend when I needed

Oscar winning actor and legendary leading man Cary Grant, with actress daughter Jennifer in the Malibu Canyon.

one. As a matter of fact, he arranged for me to audition for entrance into the American Academy of Dramatic Arts on the West Coast. He had always said that acting school might get me out of my shell. I guess he always thought I was more horse than human. Between

Me and Mr. G.

visiting Jack Klugman on the set and Mr. G's friends, I must say I have always been fascinated by acting.

So, while galloping horses, I also attended the AADA. Charlie always knew when I was in rehearsal for a play. I'd ask him if I could ride the horses that were walking "under tack" so I could study my lines. Later in my story, I'll tell you how I finally used my acting skills.

As time went by, my time in the saddle was coming to an end. You see, from the first time one gets on a horse, one thing is known—there is a piece of real estate out there with your name on it. If the gods are kind, you'll live to tell your grandkids. In my case, I ended my career in the shed row of our barn at Santa Anita.

By racetrack standards, it was not a major accident. I only had minor injuries. I tried to go back, but I realized how much my accident had affected my work. I no longer trusted horses; thus I had to leave. I had lost my heart.

Next

But I still needed a job. Los Alamitos was the first track I worked in security. It was not so bad. I could still be around the horses, but I was slowly discovering the unromantic truth of why people worked so hard with horses—so people in the grandstand could bet on them. Welcome to the real world.

Millie Vessels, who owned Los Alamitos, took a liking to me. She said that Los Alamitos never had a female in security, and she thought it would be a good idea to have one visible for her female patrons. She called the union and secured my seniority. I was later to learn that she knew she could use me in other ways as well because of my racing knowledge. A few years later, I would return her a favor. She called me into her office one day.

"I know who you are," Millie started. "You galloped horses for Charlie Whittingham."

"I did. Why are you bringing this up now?"

"Because there's a conspiracy brewing to take over my race-track."

"Who is behind it?"

"Your friend, Marje Everett."

The bulb finally went on in my brain. To this day, I don't believe the only reason she hired me was for this kind of help, but maybe she was hedging her bet for when the time came. I guess the time had come. Millie, indeed, was circling the wagons to fend off Marje.

As the weeks went on I watched Millie try her best to ward off the Everett Express and her ambition of owning all Southern California Racetracks. As history played out, we now know that Marje's dream went off into the sunset—actually it went East to Arizona.

She still keeps in touch with her close friends in Southland, but the racing scene has changed so much that one person could never dominate this giant industry.

Looking Ahead

After the Pomona Fair meet, I returned to Oak Tree at Santa Anita. About halfway through the meet, I got a call from track man Steve Wood. During the fair meet, I had met Steve and he talked about Pomona becoming an off-site training center. I told him if he succeeded, I would leave Santa Anita and go to work at Pomona. Sometime later, Steve called with some good news.

"I think we can open our off-site center. Could you come over and help?"

"Yes, I'd like that."

The head of security at Santa Anita, Dick Smith, called me into the office and told me I had first call on the job at Pomona. I told the person doing the scheduling that I wanted to work Mondays through Fridays with weekends off. When I left Santa Anita, I cried. Not only did I spend some great times there on the front side, my backside memories were unforgettable.

Working at Pomona was like starting over. Pomona was building a reputation, and I was lucky to get the opportunity to help out with getting their program going. Working with Steve Wood and using my thirty years' experience in racing, we created a pretty nice off-site training center and staved off the efforts of certain entities to shut us down.

The most important accomplishment I witnessed at Pomona was that this unassuming guy, Steve Wood, one of the most talented track men I had ever seen, was able to spread his philosophy across the state for the betterment of all horses running here. I knew he would have to move to Santa Anita, Del Mar or Hollywood Park. His was too great a talent to hide at Pomona.

I called a friend of mine in Sacramento, Sue Ross, at the CHRB and asked her if she could give Steve a consulting job. At this time, all the tracks in the state were having trouble with their surfaces and a lot of horses were breaking down. As history tells us, Steve branched out to Santa Anita and Del Mar, and across the state—and even the world. (He has tracks in other states and in South America, too!)

The fact that I was not a man never slowed me down in my racing career, nor when I auditioned for the world famous cabaret show in LA (La Cage Aux Folles.) I think this is every actor's dream, to move from yourself to an inner illusion, and then back to the character you are playing.

The character I played was Judy Garland. It was a persona I had developed in acting school. I had perfected my Garland image with the help of Lee Strasberg of Actor's Studio. I began working with him after he picked me out of a workshop at the AADA. Under him, I learned how much acting really was a part of me. It would finally serve me when I got my first paycheck at La Cage.

On any given night, I would be performing for legends like the Redgraves—Lynn, Vanessa and Lady Rachel Kempsom. The list of celebs also included Milton Berle, Gloria Estefan, Joan Collins, Barbra Striesand, Sammy Davis, Jr., and too many more to list here. Judy Garland's former husband, Sid Luft, was the constant source of my motivation. Whenever I do Judy, it's always for Sid. He is the

62

only one left who really cared. Back in the '80s, he produced a re-enactment of Judy's Carnegie Hall (starring me) and raised money for the Judy Garland/Sid Luft Scholarship at Long Beach City College. Even today, special needs kids will be able to enter LBCC and get a great education because of Sid's generosity.

Now, for you poor people who were wondering how in the hell I came up with the title for this story, it came about this way:

During one afternoon at the races, Moe (a racetrack bookie and all-around getter of things), asked me a very strange question.

"Would you like to marry Fred Astaire?" he asked.

"Why? Does he need a wife?"

"Yes, he really does."

I told Charlie about this encounter and he replied, "Mary, you mean you could have been Mrs. Fred Astaire?"

Later, Fred married jockey Robyn Smith, who had just broken up with Al Vanderbilt if I remember correctly. Robyn liked her men old! The only thing I like aged is wine.

* * * * *

The next story is based on facts from three different events in the racing world. Again, I could not name the real people in the story because most are still living. For their protection and mine, I must take the true story to my grave. As for Jaque, I still think of him when I see a French movie, and wonder what could have been. Like everyone in my life, he left something for me to hang onto—a burning passion to live life at full speed. I miss you, darling. You were the best ponyboy I ever had.

My first Judy Garland performance was at Long Beach City College where we raised funds for the Judy Garland Scholarship series. This was Sid's Judy, and he was there to give me support. Ed Lambert, VP from Capital Records, has a copy of the tape that was done that night. It was Judy's Carnegie Hall Concert, and we did it with six cameras and one intermission. Her double album won 10 Grammy's and was the first double record to do so. Someday, I would love to re-create Judy's Carnegie Hall concert to benefit AIDS research.

Author, and daytime Emmy-winner Bob Barker (host of the longest running game show, The Price Is Right) *at a fundraiser for his beloved animals.*

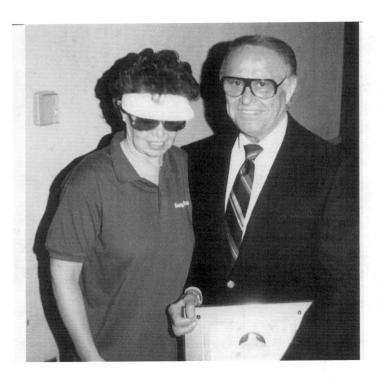

L-R The author, as pre La Cage Aux Folles Judy Garland, and award winning producer Sid Luft (one of Judy's ex's who produced the Oscar-winning movie A Star Is Born). Judy got an Oscar nomination for best actress, but Gracie Kelly beat her that year. Sid said that was the end for Judy. It must have broken her heart when she lost. To say Sid was always in the wings for me is to say he will always be in my heart. For without Sid, I could not have been Judy. He said my Judy was always the entertainer, not the Judy who lived on the other side of the rainbow . . . the side she used to call her nightmare side. I will always do the Judy that I have grown to love during my days at La Cage Aux Folles and performances at Long Beach City College and all of the other "Judy" performances that I did with my own production Company (Evening of Stars) for many charitable organizations such as Aids Research.

Author, and James Caan. Jimmy "The Cowboy" Caan (my nickname for the Godfather star) having a night out with some friends. Jimmy could horseback with the best outriders at the track. He was also a real person off the set. Never came off movie-starish. I guess that is why everyone liked him on the backside (barn area of the racetrack).

The members of the "Side Saddle Social Club" on the night of the opening of the first club ever for women on the backside of any racetrack. Thanks to Angie Dickenson and other wives of the owners in Charlie's barn, we could now bring women into jobs that once were not open to them (such as jockeys, trainers, exercise riders, grooms, hot walkers, and racing officials). I was the most proud of this legacy that I left behind when I retired. Today, you will find many women in all jobs in the racing industry.

Sales Topper

It was one of those mornings when everything I galloped, pulled. I kept hoping 10 A.M. would come quickly.

Charlie came out of the office and said, "Mary, could you go to LAX and pick up this guy who's going to visit us for a few weeks. I think this guy is a blood-stock agent from France who's here to pick up King Lamana. He's going to take him to England for stud duty." Since King Lamana was the sales topper (top seller) at the Keenland sale the year we got him, I knew he would be a great stud.

My ears perked up at the word "France". Even if this guy was a dog, he must have good taste in food and wine—something I'd missed since my last trip across the pond.

In the last couple of years, some of Charlie's owners wanted European imports. Some did well, and some are still running.

I asked Charlie what flight and airline our visitor was coming in on. Charlie handed me the information, and I was off to LAX. On arrival, I went straight to customs. Since it was an international flight, I got a drink at the bar and settled down for the long wait.

The Air France flight was coming direct from Paris, and I was thinking about the great service and food on the flight. He might not want dinner. Oh well, I'll take what I can get.

"Air France Flight 30 now clearing customs." I left the bar and went to the area adjacent to customs. Charlie told me that he had met this guy on his last trip to Paris. I was to look for a 5'7", 160-pound man with shoulder-length brown hair and brown eyes.

Well, the first fifty men fit that description, so I decided to use my "Horseman Radar" (that's how people in racing can find each other when not on the track).

A man loosely fitting Charlie's description was coming up the ramp. He stopped and began looking for someone. I prayed it was me. He was, indeed, 5'7", 150 or 160 lbs., with shoulder-length brown hair and brown eyes. And, more important, he was drop dead gorgeous! I made up my mind to be the person he was looking for, no matter *who* he was. I was even willing to tell Charlie that I missed his friend's flight.

I guess the gods shined down on me, because as I approached this vision, he looked at me and said, "Are you from the Jones' Barn?"

My heart skipped a beat. "Yes, I am. My name is Mary Bell and I gallop for Charlie. He asked me to meet you and see that you get to your hotel."

"My name is Jaque Noel. I believe you gallop a horse I sent Charlie last year. His name is King Lamana. Charlie said you did a great job. You must be very good."

I thought, "Oh no. This guy is all horses. He probably lives and breathes racing."

"Yes, I remember that horse. We won the Big Handicap at Santa Anita with him. He's a great horse."

"I'm here to set up his stud syndication."

If I had known this guy better, I'd have asked him who was going to set his syndication. I have never been shy about something I want, I don't give up until I get it. I think my mom and dad spoiled me.

I told Jaque to wait while I went for the car. He stood patiently at the curb and waited for me to return.

As I drove from the parking lot I thought about how to fix a dinner date without being pushy and how to keep him away from my girlfriends. I had a mission, and I was not ready to share. After the luggage was loaded, we began our drive.

"If you are not busy tonight, I would like you to join me for dinner," he said. YES! There is a God!

"Sure. Anything you'd like in particular? Any type of food you'd like to try?"

"I have heard of a restaurant in Los Angeles by the name of East India Grill. I have a passion for Indian food and I try to sample it everywhere I go."

His last statement knocked the wind out of me. I ate at the East India Grill at least once a month! I had discovered Indian food while in England, and had loved it ever since.

After Jaque checked in at his hotel, he asked, "Would you like to join me in the hotel bar before dinner, about seven?"

"Okay, that's a date."

As he disappeared into the elevator, our eyes locked. The last thing I remembered was his beautiful smile.

In such a short time, this man had completely overwhelmed me. I knew I was going to have to fight the urge to go faster in our new-found friendship.

In the past, I had been worse than men when it came to getting into bed. I had never been known as one who could turn down an evening of pleasure, if the sex was safe and there would be shared responsibilities if anything went wrong. This was my code of conduct. It might not fit the ladylike image I projected, but it was a crazy world. I got love where I could find it. No questions asked.

I got back to the barn, changed cars and went back to my place for a nap. I was hoping for a late night. But when I got home, I couldn't shake the feeling that my life was turning in a direction I could not control.

After my shower, I turned on some music to go to sleep by and began mapping my route to this man's bed. As sleep overtook me, I remembered the events of the day with pleasure. Did I dare think of anything other than sex with this man?

The alarm jolted me out of bed and I began the painful process of picking out an evening frock. This was not so easy. My usual garb consisted of very simple boots, pants and a shirt. Tonight, I needed more feminine attire. I searched the items at the back of the closet.

Mission complete. I stood in front of the mirror and took inventory. Not bad. My brightly colored summer dress was falling just right, and my curves were very visible. I applauded my choice.

I loved the games between the sexes. Whoever wound up winning, both received the prize.

I decided to test my dress and moves on the parking attendant at Jaque's hotel. This was not narcissistic in any way, just part of the game of attraction. You make me look. I make you look. It was a game I had played before, and armed with that experience, I hoped I could be in my new friend's bed by evening's end. I received the appropriate response from the attendant. I felt my confidence rising. I was now ready to meet my date.

I went to the bar and found Jaque at a table in the back. He was rested from his long trip and looked even more gorgeous than I'd remembered.

"Hi. Am I on time? Have you been waiting long?"

"No, you're right on time. What would you like?"

"I guess whatever you're having will be fine." Knowing he must have great taste in wine, I felt safe.

"I'm having wine. White. Is that agreeable?"

"Fine." The waiter appeared and took Jaque's order.

"I meant to tell you this morning, the East India Grill is one of my favorites. I go there often."

"That's interesting. Where did you acquire a taste for Indian food."

"When I was in England. After the races some friends took me to a place near Ascot Racetrack called Gaylord's. Were you ever there?"

"As a matter of fact, I have been there, and loved it." When he said the word *loved*, my heart stopped. It sounded so beautiful the way he smiled and said it.

I could not put any meaning to this moment, but I now found my game plan had disappeared. I would be at a great disadvantage. There was no game, no rules—just two people together. This was ground I had never been on, and I felt like a fish out of water. Never before had I been so relaxed with anyone. I simply put my brain on hold and let my heart make any necessary decisions.

After we finished our drinks and shared our mutual love of England and, of course, Indian food, we started our trip to the restaurant. I moved the conversation to the reason for his trip.

"Have you made your contacts yet?" I asked.

"I have a few owners who want to join, but nothing definite. I'll just go to some parties and talk to people. There's no hurry. I've always wanted to come to the west coast. I hope we can make a few short trips, maybe San Francisco or Monterey."

"That sounds great. Would you like to fly or drive?"

"I would prefer driving. There is more to see and enjoy."

My mind raced ahead as I fantasized a weekend in Monterey in this man's arms with the waves breaking on shore—be still my heart.

Dinner went well. I could see Jaque was pleased with the food and service. I caught myself watching Jaque's hands—how they moved with grace and how precise each finger did its job. They were long, well manicured and masculine. I began to fantasize on the pleasure his hands, put in the right places, could bring—how each touch would bring me instant satisfaction and anticipation of more.

On the drive back, I was deep in thought. Why are things moving so fast? Why can't I seem to see what's coming ahead? I guess when you let your heart guide you, your brain just gets in the way. So just sit back, go with the flow, and just let things happen.

"Would you like to have a drink in the bar before going home?"

Had I misread his signals? Was this his way of saying goodnight? I thought I'd better let my brain handle this one. My heart certainly had led me in the wrong direction. I was not ready for this eventuality. I had counted on an early breakfast.

"No thanks. I'll take a rain check. Try to be ready about 4:30. I'll pick you up on the way in." Since I lived in Santa Monica, it was not out of my way.

"I had a great time tonight," Jaque said. "I'm looking forward to the track tomorrow."

"Well, don't be surprised if Charlie puts you to work. We only entertain working guests at the barn. See you in the morning." This time I did not look back as I left, so I don't know if he even watched me leave.

As I drove home, my brain, which was now fully in operation, tried to figure out what had just happened. Was he in love with someone else? Did he have a personal rule against mixing business with pleasure?

At home I caught my image in the mirror and thought, "It only took three hours to go from the heights of erotic anticipation to the reality of rejection."

The next morning, I was not thrilled at the prospect of seeing Jaque so soon after this heart-piercing chapter in my life. But, life goes on. He was standing by the curb when I pulled up.

"Good morning," he said. "Did you sleep well?"

"Okay, I guess. I'm not used to being up that late. But, I'll catch up on my sleep later this week. How was your first night's sleep in a strange bed?" Oops! I knew I shouldn't have said that the

73

moment it left my lips. But, being spoiled and not very mature, I couldn't help myself. I felt I was the injured party and needed to let him know it.

"It looks as if I slept better than you."

That statement stopped me in my tracks. Since I did not have a response that would equal his, I settled for a draw.

The ride in was full of small talk. For some reason, I felt maybe last night was a test. With my performance this morning, I guess I flunked, but with the loss of sleep, compounded by the worst emotional let-down of my life, I was drained.

After I parked at the barn, I went straight to Charlie's office and then to the Tackroom for my morning work sheet. Charlie had me in all five sets, plus a "worker" on the turf. It was going to be a long morning.

My first horse was King Lamana, the horse Jaque had come to see. While standing in front of K.L.'s stall, I sensed someone behind me.

"Well, he looks great," Jaque said. "Charlie and you have done a great job. I know the owner, Sheik Muhammad AI-Albde, will be pleased you are sending him to stud in such good condition."

"Thanks. I love my work and I'm proud of all the horses I gallop." I excused myself and followed the groom to the middle of the "shed row," where I climbed aboard. As the set walked down the road towards the track, I looked back and saw Jaque and Charlie talking.

K.L. galloped perfectly, and the rest of the morning went the same. As the morning drew to a close, I found Jaque at K.L.'s stall talking to the groom.

"Are we done? Is it time to go?" he asked.

"Yes, we're done." We walked to the car and headed back to Jaque's hotel.

"If you're not too tired, I'd like to buy you breakfast," he offered. "Would it be out of the question to have breakfast down near the beach?"

"No, there's a nice little place near my house. But I'll have to stop first for a quick shower."

"That would be great. You're sure this won't be too much driving for you today?"

"In California, you get used to driving long distances."

Arriving at my house, I asked, "Would you like to come in, or wait for me in the Jeep?"

"I think I'd like to come in. I need to clean up a little myself."

"Do you want to shower?"

"No, I think just a small clean-up job will be necessary."

"A shower wouldn't be a problem, if you want one. You know I'd be a complete lady and respect your privacy." For some reason, he found this funny. He began to laugh, and laugh hard.

"Is that so funny?" I thought he had gotten accustomed quickly to my sense of humor.

"I'm sorry. But I have never had a woman say that to me."

I had a feeling he had experienced something like this before, but wanted to keep it to himself. I figured I would never be intimate with him, so I just put the whole encounter behind me.

When I came out of the bathroom, I noticed Jaque was at my bookcase.

"I'm sorry. I hope you don't mind. I was just looking at some of your books." He had a book in his hand. "I see you like Tennessee Williams. May I ask why?"

"I guess I liked his version of the south, the upper-class southern belles and their glove-slapping, dueling men." If I didn't know better, I would think Jaque was trying to get to know me.

"Williams is also one of my favorites. I guess the early south reminded me of some history that could have been transplanted from England." I agreed, and found his description of Williams' south to be charming.

I, in turn, was finding out more about my new friend. Only it was a very shaky start, and I had a lot of back-peddling to do. I felt like a fool. Before I even knew this man, I had put our relationship in a sexual context. I was trying to think how I could reverse the situation! How could I tell him that I was only interested in him physically and his mind was an afterthought?

I felt chauvinistic, and was not very proud of myself. Maybe, for the remainder of his visit, I should simply concentrate on showing him a good time and he would leave as a friend.

After using the bathroom he said, "I hope you don't mind me borrowing that shaving kit I found in your bathroom."

I was not surprised he used it, but surprised he would mention finding it. Was he trying to tell me he knew I had male visitors? It seemed strange that he would concern himself with my past lovers.

I almost thought of saying, "Oh, that's my brother's stuff. He visits a lot." But instead, I said, "No problem. It's been used before." Turning to the subject of breakfast on the beach, I said, "This place I had in mind is within walking distance."

"That sounds nice. Maybe a walk on the beach afterwards?"

The walk was about twenty minutes. We stopped once or twice in the great downtown area.

The restaurant was not very crowded, but Papa Louie would always have arranged a table for me under any conditions.

"Hello, my little jockey. How are you? Any good tips?"

Years earlier, I made the fatal mistake of giving Papa Louie a horse from our barn to bet on. The horse won and paid $16.20. Ever since, Papa Louie had been my best friend.

He seated us on the ocean side of the restaurant and promised he wouldn't seat anyone too close. I then introduced Jaque to Papa, and the two began a conversation in Italian. Papa lit up like a tote board. I caught a few words and knew they were talking about some town in Italy.

After a few minutes, Jaque said in English, "Well, Papa. I think my friend is hungry. What's the special for today?"

"Leave it to me. I know what she likes."

"Someday, I, too, hope to discover what she likes." Jaques said while looking at me.

I couldn't hide the blush beginning to bloom in my face.

"Thank you." How in the world was I going to survive this man's visit? I was now dealing with some serious emotions I had thought were for in my future, like falling in love and settling down. Love meant to me one person, one life. And when that time came, I would be very careful choosing my lover.

"Would you like that walk on the beach now?" I asked Jaque after breakfast.

"Very much."

I knew a quiet part of the beach where we could walk along and not be interrupted. Our conversation was small talk about racing, K.L.'s stud syndication, and England.

"Where did you learn to speak Italian?"

"My father is French; my mother is Italian. They insisted I learn both languages. They also wanted me to know their countries' histories. Growing up, I made many trips to Italy."

Jaque looked at his watch. "I'm afraid I must get back to my hotel. I have a business dinner I must get ready for. Facts and figures must be correct."

We drove back to his hotel.

"Good luck with your meeting. I hope everything goes well. I'll be thinking about you and holding a good thought."

"I'll also be holding a good thought, but not about business. See you in the morning."

*****

Santa Anita was dressed in her early morning colors of grays and oranges. As the moon gave way to the sun, the infield feast of colors began. This morning found Jaque on the pony accompanying me to the track. I didn't know if he was more concerned with K.L.'s safety or mine.

The last couple of mornings, K.L. had been getting pretty wild. Horses know when stud duty is around the corner.

Jaque jogged off with me. Then I began to gallop. Just as we passed the 1/4 pole, K.L. bucked, and off I went. Luckily, the only thing hurt was my pride. You see, I actually landed on my "pride." So after checking the damage, I looked for K.L. to see if he had hurt himself.

Spud, the outrider, had picked him up before he could get hurt. I turned around and was surprised to see Jaque racing toward me. I thought he would be helping catch the big horse.

"Are you all right? Are you hurt? Do you need the ambulance?"

"No, just bruised my pride." When I reached back and rubbed my derriere, we both began to laugh. He reached down to help me mount his pony.

"I hope this won't be an uncomfortable ride back to the barn."

"Getting dumped twice in one morning would be a legacy I'd never be able to overcome. Riding double will be no problem."

As I held Jaque around the waist, I felt my temperature rising and had trouble controlling myself. I could feel his understated strength, and could only imagine what it would be like with our bodies entwined. Before I did anything really dumb, I jumped off the back of the pony.

"We're off the track now. I can walk back to the barn from here. Thanks for the ride." For a fleeting moment I sensed that he was disappointed, or maybe that was just positive thinking on my part.

Jaque dismounted and walked with me back to the barn. This, he said, would look less embarrassing and would hide the fact that I had been separated from my mount. How considerate he was of my feelings! Our friendship was taking shape nicely.

I was given the usual greeting reserved for riders who landed on their pride on the track. "Hey, Jock, can I rub that for you or are you going to soak it all day?"

77

"Lose your horse, rider? Maybe a little glue would help?"

For some reason, Jaque thought this treatment from the guys in the barn to be unfair.

"You know, Ms. Bell is a great horsewoman and doesn't deserve your rude comments."

Even though I was flattered by this most recent show of chivalry, I had to reassure Jaque they meant no harm.

The exchange brought Charlie out of his office.

"Well, K. L.'s trying to tell us he wants to go to stud. Do you agree, Jaque?"

"Yes I do, Charlie. I think you might consider walking him a few days, under tack."

"I think I can make traveling arrangements by the middle of next week."

"And now, Ms. Bell," Charlie said. "I think you should take a little trip somewhere to rest your pride, or whatever you fell on."

"Well, I have been working hard, and getting dumped this morning should tell me something."

"Would you like to drive up the coast?" Jaque inquired. "I really would love to see this famous California coastline people talk about so much."

"Be back no later than Wednesday," Charlie added. "We have some babies coming in." It was Thursday. I figured a day and a half each way would give us at least three days up north.

"Sounds good, Jaque. Can you be ready by two tomorrow afternoon? We'll get a jump on traffic getting out of town."

"I'll be ready. I only have to make a call to reserve a space on the next cargo transport. I believe Tiger Airlines will be available, but I must call. If you call me before you leave your house, I'll be ready."

❊ ❊ ❊ ❊ ❊

On the way to Jaque's hotel, I couldn't hide my excitement. The idea of spending the next few days with him was a dream come true. I wasn't planning on our getaway as an excuse to feast on each other's bodies, but if nature overwhelmed us, so be it.

Galloping horses is a year-round, seven-day-a-week job, so it was great sleeping in for a change. I needed the extra sack time as I had not slept all that well recently. Something told me my life would change if I went away with Jaque.

I tried to figure out a way to defend my emotions. But then I decided against that ploy. I really thought I would, for the first time, just let things happen.

I got to Jaque's hotel a little after ten that morning. He was all packed and waiting for me at the curb.

"Well, traveler, are you ready for a couple of days of rest and fun in the sun?" I asked.

"Yes. I am looking forward to these next few days. Would you like me to help drive? I know you must still be sore from your fall yesterday."

"No thanks. A long hot bath took care of that little mishap. I also have been looking forward to the next couple of days. I guess I'm suffering from too much work." We both laughed.

"Now, tell me where we're going. Or should I guess?"

"The travel agent gave me a map. I guess we go up 101 to Monterey."

"You picked a very beautiful place to unwind," I said. "I've been up there a few times and it always seems to re-charge my batteries. I hope it does the same for you."

Going up 101 was a treat. Our conversation was of food, wine, and the state of affairs of Europe. Of course, racing also occupied a lot of the conversation.

"I really believe King Lamana will be a great sire. I guess when he dumped me the other day, that was his way of saying he's had enough."

"I wish you could return to England with me and help in his transition from racehorse to stud."

"I would love to, but Hollywood Park is opening in two weeks and Charlie wouldn't let me go. We have some great three-year-olds in training, and I must be at the barn every day."

We pulled into a coffee shop just outside of Malibu.

"After we get gas and eat breakfast, we should make Monterey about six, unless you'd like to stop and do some sight-seeing?"

"No, six sounds okay. We should drive straight through."

I sensed a note of urgency in his answer, almost as if he were on a timetable and had a plan he was following. Strange, for someone who was not interested in me, he sure had taken a lot of trouble arranging the weekend.

As the sun began to end its day, the coast took on different colors. For some reason, we drove the last few miles in silence, enjoying each other's company and the view.

"This drive reminds me of home on the south coast of France where my uncle and cousins live. I owe them a visit; maybe when I return."

When we reached Monterey, I asked Jaque for directions to the hotel.

"The name of the hotel is the Monterey Bay Inn. Do you know it?"

Not being able to hide my surprise, I answered, "I know it very well. In fact, I was just up here in February with an old friend."

The harder I tried to hide my great pleasure, the more amused Jaque became. "I see you are happy with my choice of hotel."

As we drove up to the hotel entrance Jaque asked, "Before we register, I must ask if you: would it be all right if we shared a room?"

BINGO! This was the nicest way a man has ever asked me to go to bed with him. I skipped a witty comeback line.

"That's fine." I prayed that the room had a king-size bed.

Jaque registered at the desk after finding me a seat in the lobby. What a discreet thing to do. It showed a lot of respect and consideration for my reputation. Little did he know, my reputation, along with my virginity, could not be saved even by the Pope.

The room was on the third floor overlooking the ocean. There was only the moon to light the night and it made the room a mirage of shadows, highlighted by a fire in the fireplace. It seemed that there had been certain instructions given, and a plan to follow.

As I surveyed the room, I felt Jaque watching me and waiting for any displeasure of mine to be corrected. I kept getting a strange feeling that Jaque had planned this weekend the day we met, and that I had judged our relationship lost too fast. Everything in my life to this point had always been get in, get out, get free. I never could figure out why I was so defensive about sharing my real emotions. I guess my mom and dad spoiled me and I never really knew how to share. After unpacking, we decided to find a restaurant.

"There's a restaurant bar on the wharf about fifteen minutes from here. How's that sound?"

"Lead the way. You make a great tour guide."

Jaque ordered, and the food and wine were very good. Again, we fell into this silence that had become so comfortable for us. Never before had I been with someone for such a short time and felt so at ease. It seemed that we had been lovers for years.

The walk back to the hotel was slow and the conversation limited to small talk. When we got back to the room, we could not find any words to say to each other.

When he took me in his arms and kissed me so softly, that answered all the questions Jaque could not answer when we first met.

As we began to feel each other's bodies, I could sense him moving along my body as if following a map—his cool hand rubbing, then holding, and finally caressing my center with his mouth. I didn't know how long it took him to get me to this point, but my head was swimming and I could not control myself. Showing my erotic pleasure so openly seemed to push him further in his desire to fulfill my needs.

For a moment, I thought, "This must be what it's like to make love to a woman. A complete partnership, appeasing one another's fantasies." For a long time, I had believed that a man was not capable of such tenderness, nor did I ever believe I would find such a man.

As the waves of satisfaction poured over me, I finally knew what Dr. Freud meant when he described an orgasm as the "little death." I guess Jaque must have made love to him, too!

When my body's appetite was fully appeased, I returned all of Jaque's kind and wonderful favors. As the final act of love was complete, Jaque and I lay side by side sharing the afterglow.

The noise of dishes woke me from my sleep. "Good Morning, Mary. How did you sleep?"

"I slept great. When did you wake up?"

"About thirty minutes ago. I thought you'd be hungry, so I called room service."

"You're sweet. I'll just have some O.J. and toast. I'm not that hungry." I looked in Jaque's eyes and saw that he had something on his mind.

"Jaque, is there something wrong? Are you upset about last night? I hope I didn't do anything you didn't want me to?"

"No, last night was one night I will never forget. But, I must confess something. Do you remember a man by the name of David Mitchell?"

"Yes, last summer. He came to Del Mar from England to ride for our barn. It was some kind of exchange program; one of our jocks went there and rode. Why do you bring his name up? What does he have to do with us?"

"I was in England, at Ascot, when David returned. He told me about Del Mar and the wonderful woman he had met and fallen in love with."

I was completely caught off guard by Jaque's story. He continued, "You must know, when David asked you to marry him and

81

you turned him down, he was devastated. Every night, David and I had dinner. He poured his heart out to me, and broke mine as well."

By now, I didn't know if David had sent Jaque on a mission of mercy, or to get even with me for saying no to his marriage proposal. I had a lot of fun with David that summer at Del Mar. But I felt marriage would never be my cup of tea. Plus, I knew there were a lot more men out there.

"I still don't know what you're trying to say, or why David should be an issue with us."

"David is an issue with us because I fell in love with you from all he told me of you. Everything David told me about you, I used to get you here, and I hoped you'd fall in love with me. From David, I learned your likes and dislikes. I knew your taste in food, wine, and what you liked in bed. Some things last night, I added myself.

"From the day I left England, I was in love with you. And when I met you, you were even better than the image I had created.

"I'm sorry if you feel I have deceived you. After we met, I was so afraid you wouldn't fall in love with me. I did not respond to your advances. Believe me, that was very, very hard. The first time I saw you, I wanted to take you to bed. It took all of my willpower not to."

For the first time in my life I was at a complete loss for words as I slowly absorbed what Jaque was saying.

"You mean you knew who I was before you met me? And you knew what food I liked, and where I like to go to get away. I thought it was strange when we headed to Monterey. This was where I had taken David for a weekend.

"So you planned everything. I don't know if I should be mad or flattered. Or maybe even a little hurt. If you know how protective I was of my real emotions, why are you trying so hard to make me fall in love with you? It didn't work for David. What makes you think it will work for you?"

I had hurt him. Like always, I said exactly what I thought. But this time, I greatly regretted it. Before Jaque could answer, I said, "Forget I said that. I'm so sorry. It's just that I spoke before my brain was in gear."

We both laughed, and the issue took on a lighter tone. This was very uncharacteristic of me. Typically I ran when confronted with a serious problem. Running kept me from ever facing my real emotions. It had always served me well—until now. Last night's encounter stripped all of that away. For the first time I was at the mercy of someone else's emotions, and I didn't know how to defend myself.

I prayed Jaque did not sense this; otherwise I was a goner. How could such a thing happen? How could I have left myself so open for feelings I didn't even know I had.

Could this be love? "Oh, no," I thought. Love is just too complicated for me. I'm not that grown-up yet.

After last night, I felt I could fall in love. Is Jaque the one, or was this a fantasy of his? Would he be gone after fulfilling his fantasy? It was going to be a long day.

"I certainly don't blame you for being upset," Jaque said. "This must have come as quite a shock. I'm very sorry I had to set a trap for you, but I don't regret doing it.

"All of the time I spent thinking about you was rewarded when we met at the airport. And it just got better. Even now, I know without hesitating that I love you and want to spend the rest of my life making you happy."

How in the hell could I respond to that?

"You're right. This has come as quite a shock to me. And I would really appreciate some time to absorb all of it. Is it possible you could give me some breathing room for now and let me think about the future?"

Jaque put his arms around me. "Of course. Take all the time you need. Please don't hold the fact I tricked you against me. Only time will show you how much I love you. Just give me a chance. You won't be sorry."

The idea of spending the rest of my life having this man love me was more than I could deal with. I pulled back from his arms.

"I'm going down to the beach for a walk, alone. Maybe not being in the same room with you, I can think a little clearer."

The beach seemed more lonely than I had remembered. I went the opposite direction of the one Jaque and I had traveled the night before. After an hour, I decided to return to the room.

"How was your walk? Did the fresh air help?"

"Not much. I guess I'll need a lot more time than this to think about us. Jaque, it's going to be impossible to spend another night together. I suggest we pack and head for home."

"If this is what you want, of course." The drive home was the longest and most painful time of my life. I simply had no idea that any man would ever affect me as Jaque had done. As we approached Los Angeles, Jaque broke a long silence.

"I guess I can only wait to hear from you. I'll be leaving for England Tuesday night. But one call, and I'll return."

"Okay, I'll call you one way or another."

I dropped Jaque off at his hotel. "I'll be at the track late to pick up King Lamana for the trip to the airport," he said, "so you don't have to pick me up. I'll ride to the track with the van people."

"Have a safe trip home, and give my love to David." This, I know, had a double meaning for Jaque. He only smiled.

Instead of going home, I thought I'd stop by the barn and check on things. I'd only been away overnight, but it seemed like an eternity.

I went from stall to stall, stopping only to visit the grooms and ask how the morning had gone. Every report was okay. I got to King Lamana.

"Rudy, when are they going to pick him up?" I asked the groom.

"I think Charlie said about eleven-thirty or twelve. I don't think Charlie is going to send him to the track. I don't think he wants to take a chance on getting him hurt. I guess he's going to be worth a lot of money at stud. By the way, where's the Frenchman you left town with yesterday? I thought you guys were going to be gone the weekend. Things didn't work out, or are you still sore from getting dumped last week?"

Rudy always had a way of getting right to the point. I guess because he was the biggest gossip in the barn.

"No, Rudy, I wasn't sore, and you're right. Things didn't work out between us."

I could see the surprise on Rudy's face. I guess he didn't expect me to tell the truth.

"Well, that's a first. Usually you use 'em, then lose 'em." Again, Rudy managed to hit the nail on the head and make me feel even worse than I already did.

"Rudy, you're right. But this time I think someone turned the tables on me. And I don't know what to do."

Rudy laughed. "You're like a kid. It's not the end of the world. See you in the morning."

* * * * *

The alarm went off, but there was really no need. I hadn't slept. For some reason it felt funny sleeping alone in that big bed. I had only slept with Jaque once, but I guess once was enough. Every time I tried to go off to sleep, I felt Jaque's body next to mine, and I'd start crying.

I told myself all that was required was a phone call and I could be with Jaque. I quickly chased any thought like that out of my mind. I must not let my heart start ruling my head. I dressed and drove to the track.

I knew I'd have to face the girls and answer the same questions Rudy had asked. "Good morning, Mary. What happened to your weekend off?" I could always count on Laura to jump at any chance to see me miserable.

"Well, Laura, it's like this. I screwed his brains out, he died, and I buried him at sea."

"Okay, Mary. If you don't want to tell us what happened, we'll understand. I mean, this is the first time we've ever seen you depressed over a man." Then Laura could not hold back laughing. "I'm sorry, Mary. It's just that you've always been so sure in your relationships with the opposite sex."

"I guess I have it coming."

We took the first set out to the "Toe" ring. Charlie looked us over and told us what to do. After the first set, Charlie could see I wasn't myself.

"Mary, come to my office at the break. I want to talk to you." Oh, no. Now Charlie is going to ask what happened in Monterey.

"Come in, Mary, and sit down. I'm not going to ask you what happened. I already know." I thought this was strange. How could Charlie know? He wasn't at the barn yesterday.

"I had a talk with Jaque last night and he told me everything. Peg and I talked about you two last night. We love you both and had really hoped you and Jaque would hit it off." Charlie could see I was getting angry. "Don't get upset."

"What do you expect me to do? I'm mad. Jaque had no right to go to you about us. We're going to work out our problems between us. He had no right. What happened in Monterey was our business, no one else's."

"Okay. Just don't run too far. You might not be able to come back."

Charlie's remark made me stop and think. For the first time, I could see Jaque and me together. I felt what Charlie had just said was more of a warning than advice.

The last set had been put away and I was cleaning my tack. I looked at my watch. It was about 10:45. I now had to make a tough decision. Leave, and not face Jaque, or stay and tell him I loved him.

Unfortunately, I chose to keep my track record perfect—I ran. And I never looked back. I got in my car and drove to the beach instead of home. I couldn't chance a phone call from Jaque. I knew if I heard his voice, I might weaken.

I walked for about two hours, hoping that Jaque would be long gone when I returned. Finally, as hard as it was, I had to return home. When I walked, in there was one message on the machine. My heart stopped. I pushed the play button. It was a hang-up. I knew it was Jaque calling to say good-bye. At least I could have been grown-up enough to face him on the phone.

I took a bath and tried to catch up on my lost sleep. About 4 P.M., I woke up and decided to go back to the barn for feed time. I went to King Lamana's stall. It was empty, and Rudy had already mucked the stall. It was finally over. Jaque and the King were gone. I began to feel a great emptiness.

Our foreman, Ed Lambert, was making his rounds.

"He left about twelve-thirty. Shipped good," Ed said. "And your friend said to say, 'Tell Mary I bought a portable phone before I left, just in case.'"

I began to cry. Thank God, Ed was there. He was probably the only one who had ever understood me.

"It's okay, Mary. Just get it all out. This must have been hard for you. You must really love this guy."

This wise old man saw what was always there, and what I couldn't see, until then.

"I think it's too late, Ed. I should have told him before he left. I don't think he'll wait for me very long. How much should I expect Jaque to put up with?"

After I ran out of tears, Ed told me to help him set the afternoon feed. Good old Ed. Always knew how to get me back to the land of the living.

The next morning, the girls saw I was still very upset and in a great deal of pain. Laura's ribbing the day before changed to concern.

"How are you doing today?" she asked.

"Numb. I can't tell you how it hurts inside. I guess this is retribution for my past relationships and how badly I've treated the men in my life. I'm really in love with Jaque, but I was afraid to tell him. Now he's gone."

"Don't kill yourself over this. I don't think it's too late. If I were you, I'd call him. We saw the way he looked at you. I told the girls, 'I think this guy won't take no for an answer.' Call him, as soon as you can. At least you'll know one way or another. But, believe me, he loves you a lot."

Before I could get to a phone, Charlie called me to his office and I could see that he was upset.

"Just got a call from the farm in England. They said Jaque and King Lamana never arrived. They said they called the airport and were told that the horse was loaded in a van and driven off."

"They weren't sure if Jaque was in the van?" My blood ran cold. "Was there any paperwork? Do they know if it was a van from the right farm?"

"I really don't know," Charlie said. "I don't even know if the Sheik knows what's happened."

"I've got his number," I said. "I'll call him now. I think it's about 10 P.M. in Oman." The call went through in just a few seconds.

"Hi, this is Mary Bell calling from California. May I speak to the sheik?" Then we waited. After several minutes I heard the sheik's voice.

"Hello, my good friend. How are you?"

"I'm fine, Mo, but I think something has happened to the King. We got a call from the farm in England, and were told King Lamana never got there. Could some of your people find out what's wrong?"

"Of course. I will call you back as soon as I know something. Do not worry. I will find out if there is wrong-doing."

"Also, a good friend, Jaque Noel, was with the King. I'm worried about his safety."

"We will make sure of your friend's safety, also."

"Thanks. You're sweet." Charlie and I waited in his office for more news. Three hours passed. Finally, the phone rang.

"Hello. This is Detective Sergeant Williams from Scotland Yard. Is Mary Bell there?"

"This is Mary Bell. Do you have news of our horse and Mr. Noel?"

"I can only tell you that the horse and Mr. Noel did arrive. But, they never got to the farm. We will have all of my office's resources at your disposal upon your arrival."

"Whose arrival? You mean me? I'm not coming to England!"

"I was told by Sheik Muhammed that he was sending his jet for you and you'd be here tomorrow."

Just as I turned around, Ed said that there were some men here to see me. "I'll get back to you. Thank you."

Outside the office, I found two of Mo's men with a limo.

"Ms. Bell, the Sheik has asked us to take you to the airport where his jet is waiting. And, he said he hoped that the gods would be with you in finding your friend."

I went back into the office to let Charlie know what was happening.

"Charlie, I'm leaving for England. Mo has sent his jet and I'm expected to be on it."

"When you see Jaque, tell him 'hi' for me."

I know Charlie was just saying that to make me feel better. I was shaking all over. What if I can't deliver Charlie's message? What if I was never to see Jaque again and tell him I love him?

Mo's men took me to my place to pack a few things. On the way to the airport, one of the men slipped me a piece of paper. It had a number on it, and the name "People in the Park."

"What's this mean?"

"When you get to your hotel, call this number. You'll know when you make the call."

Good old Mo. He had the jet waiting, and before I knew it we were in the air.

I tried to sleep the time away, but I just kept waking up thinking of Jaque and what might happen if we don't find him soon.

In his best English, the pilot said we were on approach to London. I had forgotten how beautiful the skyline was.

After landing, I went straight to the hotel. Mo had made all of the arrangements. The phone rang and I picked it up.

"Hello, this is Mary Bell," I said to the woman who answered. "I was given this number to get some information regarding a friend."

"Yes, Ms. Bell. We've been expecting your phone call. At noon tomorrow, be at the Bishop Statue at Hyde Park. Come by cab and tell the driver you want to see the Bishop."

As strange as these instructions were, I knew they would be safe to follow. The next morning I ordered a cab at the precise time.

"Where did you want to go, ma'am?"

"I want to see the Bishop," I said with an inquiring tone.

The driver turned as if to verify my identity. "Yes, Ms. Bell."

We arrived at Hyde Park about twenty minutes later and the driver directed me to the statue of the Bishop.

I sat on a nearby bench. Ten minutes later, a rather plain-looking man dressed in casual clothes sat next to me

For a minute I thought I was in some old-fashioned spy movie. He pulled out a newspaper and began to read. No, this can't be one of the people I need to make contact with. He's just too ordinary. I stared out, hoping to catch a glance from my supposed contact.

"It's all right, Ms. Bell. You don't have to look anymore."

"Oh!"

"Sorry to startle you. Please relax."

"I'll try. This is difficult for me." I took a very deep breath. "Okay, I'm fine now."

"I understand you are trying to find someone."

"Yes, I am. I'm also trying to find the horse he left California with. Can you help?"

"I represent a consultant group that specializes in property recovery. Give me as much information as possible."

I answered his questions as best I could.

"What do I need to do next?"

"We'll contact you when the property is to be returned." He sounded confident, almost as if he already knew where Jaque and the King were.

"That's fine. So, I'll just go back to the hotel and wait, right?"

"Yes, Ms. Bell. That's what you do, and please don't talk to anyone about our meeting. It could get your property damaged."

This guy was too much. First he tells me in no uncertain terms that everything is okay. Then he scares me to death.

"I'm sorry, but I forgot to ask you about your fee."

"Someone will be at your hotel later to give you an estimate on your property. They will identify themselves to you as an associate of the People in the Park." He slipped away, and I took a cab back to the hotel. This driver treated me like any ordinary fare.

I stayed in my room, fearful that I might miss any message that they might send. Besides, the trip had taken a lot out of me. For dinner, I ordered something French, just for old times' sake.

When my head hit the pillow, I went out like a light. I had no idea how much time had passed when I was awakened by a knock at the door.

"Who is it?"

"Someone from the park," a woman's voice answered.

A statuesque woman of incredible beauty stood in the door-way—very tall, with golden blond hair and powder blue eyes. Her smile was confident and assured. Her clothes complemented her perfect curves. When she entered the room, she did so cautiously, as if she had police or military experience. With her surveillance complete, she settled on the couch.

"Would you like a drink?"

"Yes, please."

"Wine is all I have. Will that do?" She nodded.

I poured what was left in the bottle from my dinner. She sipped her wine with the elegance of someone who was used to fine wines.

"I understand you're from California," she said after a few moments.

"Yes, I am. Santa Monica, to be exact. Have you ever been to California?" She changed the subject.

"The group has asked me to inform you that the recovery fee will be one million dollars."

She said that, I believe, with the knowledge of what could have been a ransom demand made earlier.

"I'll contact my people and find out if that's acceptable. Can you call me back, say about eleven tomorrow morning?"

"Agreed."

Why did I think that if I asked her to stay the night, she might knock a few dollars off? If I weren't so head over heels in love with Jaque, I would have tried. I felt she wanted an invitation. But the only thing she got that night was wine.

When she left, I called Mo with the news.

"Go to the desk in the morning," Mo said. "The money will be wired to you. Please do not try and help. These people are mercenaries. I have used them before. They will get the job done, but you don't want to know how."

"Mo, I don't want any part of these people. I understand. I won't get involved. But it will be hard not knowing what's happening."

"Be patient. You must have faith. You will see your lover again soon. Trust your love for him, and you will be united."

"Thanks, Mo. You're a great friend, and you understand me so well. But how did you know I was in love with Jaque?"

"When you called me from California, you said you needed my help finding your friend, and then you said, as an afterthought, and King Lamana. That was the first time I'd ever heard you put a human life before that of a horse."

I turned off the lights and tried to go to sleep. So many things were going through my mind. What if they can't find Jaque and K. L.? What if I never get a chance to tell him I love him?

✴ ✴ ✴ ✴ ✴

"Good morning, Ms. Bell. This is the desk. I'm sorry to wake you, but you have a money wire at the desk."

"It's fine. I was expecting it. I'll be down in a few minutes."

The wire was in the form of a bank draft. The only thing missing was my signature.

Seeing a million dollars didn't impress me. Mo had sent me all over the world with much more money to buy his horses. This was, nevertheless, a very important million dollars. It could make the difference between life and death for Jaque.

I felt so useless. I felt that I should be able to do something to help them. Maybe they don't know how to take care of a horse. Not everyone knows how to muck a stall or groom a horse.

It's funny what things rush through your mind when you're scared. I wished I had the last week to live over. I would have done things differently. I certainly would have made Monterey a lot more enjoyable for Jaque. To this point, I thought life was a game and I played by only one rule—mine. Now I know that was selfish of me. Life was meant to be shared.

I broke my train of thought to answer the phone.

"Mary, this is Mo. Have you heard anything?"

"No, I haven't, but I got your wire. I guess all I can do now is wait."

"You must keep faith. Allah will be merciful; his wisdom is not to be questioned. One way or the other, it is destiny."

"Thanks for the kind words, Mo. They'll help get me through a few hours. I've been going through some very tough times lately. When all of this is over, I'll never take another person's feelings for granted."

"I'll pray for your friend."

"Thanks."

* * * * *

The fourth morning came, and with it another restless night. I turned on the TV to catch up on events.

"Police today found five bodies in a farmhouse ten miles from Kent. Scotland Yard has discovered that these persons might have been victims of a bomb.

"Authorities are now speculating that the men were making bombs and the bombs accidentally detonated, killing all five.

"There is speculation that the men were tied to a group of terrorists working out of the Middle East.

"An investigation is underway to determine who they were targeting here in England."

I found it poetic justice that the dumb bastards blew them-selves up. If someone was holding Jaque hostage, I wish they'd do something equally dumb so this would be all over.

The day passed and still no word. I turned on TV for the afternoon news.

"On a follow-up note from this morning's reported bombing, Scotland Yard has determined that the men killed in the bombing died at their own hands. The Yard could find no evidence to deter-mine their intended victims, if any. This, according to police spokes-man, Chief Inspector Williams."

Williams! He was the officer who phoned me in Charlie's office. Could these guys have something to do with Jaque, or was it just a simple coincidence? Just then, the phone rang.

"Mary?"

"Yes."

"Go to the front of the hotel and wait there. You'll be con-tacted." The line went dead.

I stood by the curb watching cars darting in both directions. So many people going about their normal business, and I stood there not knowing what would happen to me next.

A very ordinary looking car pulled up and a man got out.

"Mary Bell?"

"Yes, I'm Mary Bell."

"Come with us, and please, no talking." I nodded. The man followed me into the back seat, and another man drove. We drove out of the city.

"Don't be alarmed, but for your own safety I must blindfold you. Security, you understand." Like I had a choice in the matter.

About an hour had gone by. The car stopped and I heard low voices.

"Okay, Ms. Bell. I'm going to walk you to the barn. Then I'll take your blindfold off. Please follow all instructions to the letter. Your life could depend on it."

I felt a hand on mine, and then the voice of a woman.

"Hello, Ms. Bell. I'll take you from here." It was the woman who came to my room that first night. Her touch was soft and confi-dent. "Just let me lead you. Don't try and walk alone."

Since this was my first time in a blindfold (outside the privacy of my bedroom), I was having trouble walking. But the woman had a great deal of patience and never lost her temper. I could tell I was passing through a doorway.

"I'm going to take off your blindfold now."

It took my eyes a few seconds to get used to the light.

"Please follow me."

We walked over to a stall that was covered in front by a sheet. She removed it, revealing a horse.

"Is this your missing horse?" I checked his mouth. All race-horses have a tattoo on their lip for identification. I had remembered K.L.'s because I held him the day he got his tattoo. It was K.L.

"That's the horse. The tattoo confirms it."

"Thank you. Now, we're going to put the blindfold back on. Please, no talking."

"Where's Jaque? Is he safe? Please tell me."

"Ms. Bell, you'll be told on a need to know basis only. Please, no talking. Also remember, this trip never happened."

My blindfold was put back in place and I was returned to my hotel. The phone was ringing when I entered my room.

"Be downstairs at the curb in twenty minutes with the money." I prayed this meant their job had been successful.

This time when a car pulled up, there was only one man in it. He leaned over the passenger's side.

"Ms. Bell, please get in."

I assumed that the "no talking" rule was still in effect. The man never said a word, so I kept quiet. We drove to Hyde Park.

"You can get out now. Go to the statue of the Bishop. Some-one will contact you."

I sat by the statue for what seemed like an eternity. I wasn't scared, but very anxious, so the time seemed to drag. Typical London fog began to cover the park. I could only think of Jaque coming back. After the events of the last couple of hours, I hoped it all would be over in the next few minutes. I kept checking the money to see if everything was in order.

I had been sitting in the park for at least an hour when I heard footsteps. First, I could only see a shadow. But as it came closer, I realized it was Jaque! I started to run to him.

"Stop! Don't get any closer," a voice boomed out of the fog. Jaque also stopped.

"Ms. Bell. Put the envelope back on the bench and walk to-wards the east end of the park. That will be to your left."

I tried to determine where the voice came from, but with the fog that was impossible.

When I turned back to see Jaque, he was gone. What kind of game were these people playing now?

I left the envelope on the bench and began to walk east. The fog was not as bad in the east end of the park. I finally came to the street, where a cab was waiting. I took it for granted the cab was there for me, and simply got in. The driver took off, and I was too upset to notice we were not headed back to the hotel.

Suddenly, the driver pulled over to the curb, got out and opened my door. As I got out, I looked at where we were and began to cry. It was Gaylord's, and my driver was Jaque!

"Sorry, ma'am. I must've taken a wrong turn."

I put my arms around him and held him so tight I thought he'd turn blue.

"Funny thing happened on the way to the farm. Shall we get some dinner? I've got a lot to tell you." He took off the cabbie's hat and jacket, and we went in and got a table in the back.

"Are you okay? Did you get hurt? I was so worried about you."

"Just a couple of bruises. I'll explain later. Let's order. The two thoughts that kept me going were of you and Indian food."

We both laughed and it felt so wonderful. Over the past few days I had forgotten what it was like to laugh. His laugh was the same as always, full of life. I had missed that.

Jaque ordered some "stones" and ginger wine, and began his story.

"When we landed in England, the customs people came out to the plane. They said the vet would be out in a few minutes. We stood by as two men pulled up a van and said, 'Load the horse in the van and we'll take it to its quarantine stall.'

"Okay, should we follow?'

"No, you come with us in the van and we'll give you the horse's paperwork. Then, if you'd like, we'll get you transport to the hotel of your choice.' I didn't think anything was out of order.

"These men seemed like they knew what they were doing. They were certainly very nice and accommodating. When I think about it now, I should have been suspicious. Government officials aren't really that efficient and friendly."

The food arrived and Jaque continued.

"Then, as I got into the van, I soon realized these men were not vets. We drove out the other side of the airport where they had cut down part of the fence. When we got to the street, three men in another van were waiting. I asked what was happening and one of the men said, 'No talking' and he pulled a gun.

"I shut up, and the next thing I knew another man put a blindfold on me. After that, there's not much I can tell you. We finally got to an old farm and they told me to take care of the horse.

"When we got inside the barn, they took off my blindfold and showed me where I was to sleep and groom the horse. I really never thought about getting away. I didn't want to leave K.L. in their hands, whoever they were. And I don't think they knew how to take care of him. I guess that's what saved me. Even now, I have no idea who these five men were."

A bell went off in my head.

"Did you say *five men?*"

"Yes, five."

"It could be just a coincidence, but yesterday the news reported that five terrorists accidentally blew themselves up."

"I didn't hear any explosions, but yesterday about one in the afternoon, two other men and a woman came into the barn, asked who I was, and the name of the horse.

"For some reason, I knew that these were the good guys.

"What had happened to the men who had kidnapped me and the horse,' I asked them.

"The woman answered, 'You don't have to worry about them anymore.'

"They took me to a car and drove me to a hotel where I could clean up. Then, they dropped me off at the park, asked me to identify you and then wait in the cab. They said I was free to drive off anywhere and take you with me. That's when I thought about coming here."

"These people who rescued you, did they say anything else?"

"Come to think of it, the woman said something strange. She said, 'Mr. Noel, you are a lucky man. You have someone who loves you very much. I hope you treat her right.' That's all that was said. I guess the way these people operate, we'll never know what really happened the last few days."

"The most important thing is you are safe and K.L. will soon be starting his life as a sire . . . Oh, my God!"

"What's wrong?"

"I didn't call Mo and tell him everything was okay." I excused myself and went to the phone.

"Hello. This is Mary Bell. I need to talk to the Sheik." Mo's voice came on.

"Hello, my friend. I know your good news. I have just heard myself. The farm called, verifying K.L.'s arrival. You must now be having dinner with your friend, right?"

"You are a very wise man, Mo."

"With years, you too will be wise, my friend. I hope your reunion will be a fruitful one."

"You can count on it."

I returned to the table and told Jaque the good news.

"Maybe before you return to the States, you can go out to the farm with me and say good-bye to K.L.? If I remember rightly, you weren't there at the barn to say good-bye when we left California."

I knew Jaque was posing his question in such a way that I could answer in more than one way.

"Well, I was thinking I'd better stick around a while and gallop K.L. You know, help him get settled. I certainly owe Mo that much. He saved the life of the man I love."

"Is this your way of saying you'll marry me?"

"Are you asking?"

"Yes, Mary Bell. Will you marry me?"

"Yes, my darling, I will."

We finished our dinner in silence.

La Cage

In "I Could Have Been Mrs. Fred Astaire," I touched on my life at La Cage. This side trip was more of a journey into a life I had to live to believe. It all started with seeing an advertisement in the *L.A. Times*.

"Auditions every Tuesday at La Cage for the most beautiful men in the world." Reading on, I found that the performers were playing famous singers. Since I did a super Judy Garland (this was born out of my AADA days), I decided to show up, and the rest in history. From 1989 to 1990, I was the real *Victor, Victoria*.

To the boys, the money was good and the life was pure Real Girl stuff. Clay Norse was the creative genius behind the show at La Cage. He never got much credit, but everyone knew he was our backbone. He did Barbra Streisand, Bette Midler, and whoever came in that night. Clay also made my Judy come alive. He was my inspiration and found priceless one-of-a-kind Judy songs for me to wow the countless audiences. Along with Paul Fisher's great hair, and make-up, I took many people back to those days when Judy could take an audience to her heart and find that elusive rainbow.

Author as Judy Garland. An acting job that took me from woman . . . to man . . . to Judy Garland. If that is not an actor's dream, I don't know what is. I guess I was the real Victor/Victoria *(no offense, Julie A).*

One song comes to mind. When our producer was out of town, we were like kids left alone in a candy store. We were left to create our own numbers. Of course, everyone ran to Clay and Paul for help. It was Easter, and Clay gave me the famous movie *Easter Parade* song. The thing he didn't tell me was that the whole cast was going to join me on stage. This was never allowed because the cast was always between numbers for costume changes.

To say I was taken aback is an understatement. The boys not only filed on stage, they were all wearing hats that I could never describe in a million years. I held up great until our flamboyant MC, James "Gyspy" Haawk, slowly came to center stage with a huge

Author as Judy Garland, with Emmy-winning star Milton Berle after a show at La Cage. When Uncle Miltie said you passed, then you passed, and you became a member of La Cage. He knew I was a woman, and got a kick out of the way I pulled off being a man . . . night after night.

watering can on his head surrounded with every flower he could find in his garden. I was so glad we had our friends from Japan there that night. I think any other audience would have walked out.

Skip and Wally were our technical staff. Skip made all of Paul and Clay's ideas reality, and Wally was a lighting whiz. Between them, our show was spectacular. The boys were always allowed to

Author, and Grammy-award-winning singer/actor Gloria Estefan posing for a La Cage photo after a show.

Actor Joan Collins, and author as Judy Garland. One day at the track, John Forsythe introduced me to Joan, and till this day I don't believe Joan recognized me at La Cage. The one thing I remember about Joan is that she always had her daughter with her. After her daughter's accident crossing Rodeo Drive, Joan was at her side every chance she could. Joan is a great mom. Many other Hollywood moms could use her as a role model. She loved my Judy . . . because she saw Judy in England.

Author, with another cast member of La Cage, Clay Norse. Clay did all of my Judy numbers (and for that matter, he did all of the La Cage numbers). Along with Skip (sound man), and our lighting genius, Wally, Clay did some great things on stage at La Cage. I miss him a lot.

create from within. I believe Clay is retired and Paul has his own salon in Vegas (still working his magic on the ladies of the fabulous desert hotspot).

One man who comes to mind was the award-winning Busty O'Shea, whose act always stole the show. He would create numbers that would bring down the house. Along with Gypsy, Busty did outside TV and movies.

Gypsy was our light of lights. He brought the audiences to their feet with a simple wave of his hand. More notably, he was nominated for best supporting actor in his very first movie, Mel Brooks' *To Be, Or Not To Be.* La Cage closed in the late '90s, and Gypsy is now doing a lot of TV. He is still going strong.

But if I had to pick one man who stood out in the show, it would have to be Bobby Etienne. He was a master of illusion. He *was* the women he was performing. Tina Turner once said of Bobby, "He does me better than I do myself."

Anita Baker came to La Cage, and walked away talking to herself. She said, "If I didn't see it with my own eyes, I would not have believed it."

Many celebs graced out showroom. Some I found nice, and some I found to be off their rockers. It would serve no purpose to list the good and bad of Gay Hollywood. Their lives will DRAG them down (pardon the pun) eventually.

James "Gyspy" Haawk before, and after make-up. He was nominated for an Oscar for his role in the Mel Brooks comedy To Be or Not To Be. He was world-known as our La Cage MC. Stars like Lana Turner and many, many more would come to the show just to be "dished" by him. It was a riot to see Hollywood's biggest and brightest on the other side of the footlights.

Another cast member of La Cage that I shared many great moments on stage with was Busty O'Shea. He was entertainer of the year in Las Vegas and Atlantic City, a great actor who did a lot of TV and movie work.

Another cast member from La Cage, Bobby Etienne. Bobby was a real girl, and could have been a great lesbian . . . if only I could have talked him into losing that extra weight downstairs.

Emmy-winning actor Alan Rachins star of LA Law and *Dharma & Greg,* and author (in Judy Garland make-up). He came to La Cage one night and asked me to help with his make-up. He was opening in the stage production of La Cage Aux Folles in Florida at the Burt Reynolds dinner theater.

Second from left: Anna Mae (Tina Turner). She was my first body-guard job, but it turned out to be more of a baby-sitting thing. Many things have been said about Tina Turner, but the most important thing I could say about Miss Anna Mae is that she is a super mom . . . in the tradition of Jackie Kennedy.

L-R: Rappers "Warren G", and his cousin Jeffery ("Snoop Doggy Dog") during a music video shoot. That same year, I had the Dalai Lama to look out for. It was a strange year, to say the least. But don't shoot the messenger for sending the message. Jeffery and Warren are just urban storytellers, and their story is worth hearing. Also hats off to another friend (not pictured) in the rap community—Joe Simmons, who is a real voice from the heavens . . . see you in church.

Diary of an All-Season Hunter

The last side trip I took was as a BRA (Bail Recovery Agent). In the days of the wild west, we were called bounty hunters. Today, with the help of PCs, we hunt with a laptop, not a .45. Bob Burton was my mentor. With his training I have managed to stay alive. the following comes out of a diary I kept over the last few years.

Bob Cue (IASP) was the first person to put a gun in my hand. And for the last thirty years his friendship has meant a lot to me. Besides showing me how to shoot a gun, he taught me why I needed to respect the weapon that was in my hand. He is a great American, and someday I hope to follow in his footsteps . . . the footsteps of a true hero. The names and dates in the following have been changed for obvious reasons.

People vs A.J. Singh

On the morning of July 6th, a bench warrant was issued for A.J. Singh for failure to appear to answer one count of first-degree murder. After getting the paperwork from the bondsman, I began my investigation. I had a strong hunch that this Jump would try to go back to India.

"If this Jump gets out of the country, do you want me to spend the money to bring him back," I asked the bondsman.

"I'll spend as much money as it takes to get this guy back," he said. "He killed his own son."

Bondsmen usually don't let their feelings get in the way of business. But his wife had just given birth to their first child—a boy. I guess this made it personal.

"I'll bring this Jump back in a box if you want me to," I offered. This guy gave me a lot of business and I wanted to assure him that I was committed.

"No, just bring him back so he can spend the rest of his life in prison thinking about what he's done."

I ran his cards and found a ticket to Bombay. I booked the next flight out and was in India the next day.

In India, money talked and bullshit walked. I didn't waste anytime throwing money around. I found out that the Jump's brother had been killed in a political uprising. Then, when I read that the dead brother's daughter was getting married in Goa, not far from Bombay, I took a train to Goa and waited. I was hoping that the Jump would show up to give the bride away.

I was right. The guy was there, and after the wedding was over, I walked up to him and told him I would be taking him back to Los Angeles for trial.

By his expression, I could tell that he was thinking about taking off. He was a big guy, and I thought I'd have to kill him to bring him back. But I remembered that the bondsman wanted this Jump to rot in prison. I had hired a couple of locals to help. I told the Jump to look over his shoulder and think twice about running.

I didn't have any trouble with the local authorities because I told them that this guy had killed his own son. They felt that he deserved whatever was waiting for him in the States. It seems that boys are prized in India, and killing them is not looked upon very nicely.

Taking him along the way was tough. England was easy, but getting through New York to Los Angeles was a bitch. After finally arriving, I asked for the PD to take him off the plane at the tarp.

The PD were waiting for me, and they were a sight for sore eyes. I've gone long distances with Jumps, but not with such a cold-hearted killer as this guy was. Later, I found out that he got life with no parole.

People vs Leo Campbell and Raider

On March 17th, a bench warrant was issued for a non-appearance by Leo Campbell and his dog, Raider. This was a very different case for me. The Jump had fled the state because his dog had bitten someone and he was afraid the court would order his dog destroyed.

The Jump lost his home, quit his job, and began running from state to state. It was almost an impossible task hunting this pair down. By the time he used an ATM in one city, he was on his way to the next. The clock had only two weeks left when I caught up with him and his dog.

I decided to grab the dog, hold it hostage, and make the Jump come to me. While observing the front yard of the house where the Jump was staying, I saw the dog come out the front entrance and into the yard.

I coaxed the dog into my car, drove to the nearest police station and phoned the Jump. I told him that he could have his dog back for a hundred bucks. I told him to meet me at a bar—that just happened to be next door to the police station. I heard later that the Jump paid his fines and settled the lawsuit.

He and Raider later moved to a cabin in the Colorado mountains where, I assume, they lived happily ever after. This is a case where a dog's best friend was a man!

People vs Diana Ross

I am what I am. And what I am needs no excuses.

While vacationing in New York, I ran into a fellow Hunter. "I have paper on a Jump I think is headed west," he said. "If you're headed home soon and are interested in looking the guy up in L.A., you can have half of the bond."

"As a matter of fact, I'm leaving in the next few days."

"Interested in half?"

"Sure. What's the story?"

He told me he had an early clock, my timing would be fine, and he filled me in on the details.

Once I got home, I started calling the bars in West Hollywood, especially the ones that offered female impersonators. It seems this Jump, himself an impersonator, owned half of a club in New York and ran off with all the money—about 250 grand! The partner filed criminal charges. Then, after he was arrested, that same partner put up his bail!

This guy impersonated Whitney Houston, Grace Jones and the great Diana Ross. Do you have any idea how many Diana Rosses there are in West Hollywood? A lot.

I found out that a new queen had come into town and had put a touring company together. They performed at gay clubs in various cities. I picked up a flier advertising the next show, hoping that this guy and my Jump were the same. The guy was hard to ID because I had his booking photo, and he wasn't Diana Ross.

I arrived early, threw some money around, and asked to see the club owner. I posed as a booking agent interested in hiring the group. After the show, the owner introduced me to the guy I hoped was my Jump. He was in costume, so I couldn't really make an identification.

I made a lunch date to sign the papers to hire his troop. The closest restaurant I could think of near the men's jail was Felipe's. I knew that this guy wouldn't dare show up in drag, so I could make sure he was my man—if you'll pardon the expression.

At the restaurant, the first words out of the guy's mouth were, "I hear you want to book me."

"Truer words were never said," I replied, and we booked him at the nearby jail.

And yes, he was every man's woman. I heard they extradited him back to New York.

Now when anyone asks me about my most interesting Jump, I can say with a straight face, "Well, I guess the day I arrested Diana Ross at Felipe's was the highlight of my 25-year career."

People vs Jessie White

On the morning of November 22nd, a bench warrant was issued for Jessie White for failure to appear in court to answer one count of assault and battery. Since this was the third strike on his record, he was going to be hard to bring in.

After getting the paperwork from the bondsman, I began my investigation. The Jump was using his girlfriend for money and a little nooky. I tried to stake out her house, but it was impossible. The guy came and went at different hours. If I stayed very long I would quickly give myself away.

So I went down to the local Chevy dealership and asked one of the salesmen to drive a new Corvette to the girlfriend's place and try to convince her that her guy had won it. The manager of the dealership okayed the set up, and the plan took shape.

I knocked on the door and the girlfriend came out. She was pretty sharp. I knew I'd have to show her some proof that this was really her boyfriend's car. I told her that we got the boyfriend's name from his credit card. Since I had subpoenaed his records, I showed her a copy of her card. She bought the story.

"Can I sign for him?" she asked.

"No, the rules specifically state that he has to personally claim the car within 24 hours or we have to award it to the runner up."

"Well, I might be able to find him today," she suggested. "Where will the car be if I do?"

I told her the name of the dealership, and had the salesman drive the car back to the lot. I could only wait and hope that this guy's greed overtook his desire to stay out of prison. I didn't have long to wait.

The Jump showed up at the dealership a few hours later. The manager phoned me and I was there in record time. I walked up to the Jump, identified myself, and booked him into the local PD.

People vs Terri Carter Wilson

Helping Hand

On the morning of June 6th, a bench warrant was issued for Terry Carter Wilson for failure to appear in court to answer one count of first degree murder. After getting the paperwork from the bondsman, I began my background check.

I found out that she had two kids and that they were staying at her mother's house in San Diego. I waited there patiently for her to show, and she didn't disappoint me. As she walked up the driveway of her mother's house, I saw her kids running out to great her.

I felt that this would be a moment when she would be off guard. I walked up, identified myself, and told her that I would be taking her back to Los Angeles for trial. The look in her eyes told me everything I needed to know about this very kind lady.

As a BRA, you get to know who you are hunting. This woman was not a murderer. On the way back to Los Angeles I asked her about the crime.

"Why did you kill your husband?"

"He was constantly beating me. I didn't know what else to do."

"You had other options, you know. You could have called the police at any time."

"I didn't think that the police would believe me. I was afraid if I left, he would hunt me and the kids down and kill us."

I wound up testifying for her in court as a character witness. This was the first time I had ever testified for any Jump. I heard later that she got help from the court and that the D.A. had reduced her charge to manslaughter. She served two years, was released, and is now living with her children and mother in San Diego.

The old saying that the guilty always run is not always true. Sometimes people don't understand the justice system and don't understand that they can get help. Killing her husband was not the answer, but it seemed like the only way out for her.

People vs Perry King

The One That Got Away

On the morning of April 8th, a bench warrant was issued for Perry King for failure to appear in court to answer 25 counts of embezzlement and fraud. After receiving the paperwork, I began my investigation. I knew if this guy was smart enough to steal 50 million bucks from all of these people, he sure as hell could duck me for 90 days. I knew I had my work cut out for me.

I ran his last credit card records and found out he bought a plane ticket to South America. This meant that I had a long chase on my hands.

Once down in South America, I located the local information guys. The price wasn't that high to find out where this guy was. I guess things were slow down there. A little money would take me a long way.

I found out that he had bought into a coke club. I got a sickening feeling that my trip was over. I knew if this guy had gotten to the right people, they would protect him well. There would be no way I could get him out. If I tried, they'd probably find my body in a shipment of bananas headed for the South Pole.

I called the bondsman with the bad news. "Come on back," he told me. "It isn't worth your life to bring this guy back."

Just before I left, I started a little rumor about the new American in town. I said he had come down to take over the coke club. I hoped to capitalize on the paranoia of these locals so they would take care of this guy.

After I was back about a week, I read about how this guy fell out of a helicopter while sightseeing over the Amazon. I guess some kind of justice was served, but it didn't get those poor people their money back.

People vs Dr. Alex Collins

Dr. Jekyll and Mr. HIDE

On the morning of July 10th, a bench warrant was issued for Dr. Alex Collins for failure to appear to answer multiple counts of child molestation. After getting my paperwork from the bondsman, I began my background investigation.

I subpoenaed his ATM and all credit card records. I also asked the bank to flag his account so I could find out his location when he needed money. I got the records back from the last card used, a department store in the Beverly Center.

I went to the manager of the men's store that showed on the card. He took me to the department where the last purchases were made. Collins had purchased warm weather clothes, so I had a couple of states to start with—New Mexico, Arizona and Nevada.

Then the bank called and said that the Jump had just withdrawn a thousand dollars at a Las Vegas casino. I was on the next plane.

Once there, I called a couple of friends at some of the casinos to ask if they had done any recent hiring. It was a dead end. This Jump couldn't apply for any job that required a background search.

From what I knew about child molesters, they never can be rehabilitated. So I began to call some of the schools in the area. Vegas turned up nothing, but nearby Henderson turned up as a possible. A guy matching the Jump had hired on as a handyman.

I went to the school, told the principal about the Jump, and showed him a photo. The principal identified the Jump, and I found him in the break room having his lunch. I told him I was taking him back to Los Angeles for trial. Before I left, I contacted the local PD and told them to check with the kids to find out if the guy had molested anybody at their school.

Fortunately, he hadn't done any damage there. Seated in the plane coming home with this guy took all the self-control I had. I wanted to ask the pilot if he could open the door so I could throw this guy out over the desert.

A Blow Job or Blow Your Head Off

A l Segal called me one evening and asked if I wanted to work a Jump with him and his posse. I never missed a chance to work with this living legend, so I quickly agreed. "It's going to be in a bar," Al said, "so be sure to wear something sleazy."

Al always sent me in to ID the Jump and then get the guy outside with the promise of a BJ. This always worked. It was fun working with Al, a retired LA detective who got tired of seeing his collars walk. This was the best way to get even with the bad guys without getting in trouble with Internal Affairs. Al taught me so many things that saved my ass on more than one occasion. I'd walk through fire to get a Jump for Al, and I know he would do the same for me.

This night started out routine enough, but when I went to the ladies room to pretty myself up, I found I wasn't alone. A couple of the local girls asked me to work the other side of the city, and I think they were about to stress this point with a six-inch knife.

I had no way of calling for help, so I just played tough. In one move I pulled out my two-inch colt and said, "If you girls just let me finish my business here, I will go and never work this bar again." Then I put my gun to the head of the closest girl and waited.

They agreed to my terms and I went back to the bar. I found Al's Jump at the bar with about ten guys standing guard. They let me through to make my pitch. I told him five dollars for the BJ, an offer he couldn't turn down.

I knew his army would not follow him out. If the guy didn't blow his wad, he wouldn't want his buddies to see his dick go limp. Out behind the club, I told him to get in my van. Al was waiting with his posse to take him into custody.

After the smoke cleared, Al said, "Everything went off okay. Right, Mary?"

"Sure Al, but don't ask me to work this side of town again for a while."

"Why?"

I smiled. "I think the ladies in the ladies' room ain't no ladies," I replied.

People vs Raymond Cruiz

S.O.S.—Save Our Son

On the morning of March 12th, a bench warrant was issued for
Raymond Cruiz for failure to appear in court to answer two
counts of second-degree manslaughter. After getting the paperwork
from the bondsman, I began my background investigation.

Since the Jump's mother and father put up their house for the
bond, I began with them. Mexican Jumps were always the hardest
ones to bring in because they usually headed south of the border to
hide out with other family members. I didn't have much hope in
making the clock.

I showed up at the boy's house to interview the parents. Before
I could say anything, the mother began to tell me that she wanted
me to find her boy first. She feared the police would shoot him down,
and she was right. The boys in blue have a way of shooting first and
never asking questions later.

She added that the two boys her son killed were in a rival gang, and they would also be looking for him. I guess she felt that I would bring her boy back in one piece. The only problem was that I got most of my information about street Jumps from gang members. If I were to start asking around about this boy, they would try and take me out to eliminate any competition. I told the mother to contact me the minute she heard from her boy.

About two days later, the mother called and told me where her son was hiding: a motel on Pacific Coast Highway in Long Beach. I phoned his room, told him that I had a plan, and cautioned him to not leave the room. He told me that he saw a couple of lookouts that he thought were from the rival gang.

"Stay put!" I ordered. "I'll get there as soon as I can" I remembered that there was a nightclub called Angles not far from the motel. I had a friend who worked there, so I called and asked her if she could help.

"It might be dangerous," I warned.

"Mary, I work a topless bar. It's great training to become a karate master. There isn't much I haven't seen or done."

"All right then, have your girls ready about nine tonight."

After picking up the girls from the club, I headed towards the motel. When I pulled up, I opened the van and the girls jumped out—topless, of course, with tits flapping in the wind. The gang lookouts were so busy looking that I got into the boy's room and got him out before anyone knew it.

About ten minutes later, I booked the boy at LBPD, then called his parents and told them the good news. I went back to the club, paid the girls and thanked them. This was yet another example of sex or greed doing in the bad guys. It works every time.

✷ ✷ ✷ ✷ ✷

It's hard to end this book. It has taken 50 years to live it, and seven years to write it. Some things I will keep to myself, unless some fast-talking talk show host can pry more facts out of me. I only hope in reading this that you find in yourself some of life's lessons I have learned.

Cary Grant was great at bringing out the best in anyone he liked. My life with him set the stage for all of my side trips. But the real heroes of my story were my mom and dad. Jim and Alice had a baby girl, but wound up with a jockey, exercise rider, actor, performer, bodyguard, and bounty hunter, as well as a loving daughter.

Their never saying no gave me the courage to do all of the crazy things I have done in my life. My dad is in heaven now, and my mom is just hanging around until she can join Dad and they can finish that 50th anniversary they missed by only a couple months. I know the first thing my dad will ask my mom when she joins him is, "What in the hell has Mary gotten herself into now?"

Author at three months . . . waiting for the photographer to get the bloody picture taken. As you can see by the other pictures in this book, I learned to have a lot more patience, in posing for pictures. And of course, I have added clothes.

Author, and brothers Mike and Pat. Through their eyes I could see for miles, for they took me where they went. Through their hearts I could see the love and the light of others. For my father taught us all that we are not alone, and we must love or lose . . . and it was never an issue whom we chose to love.

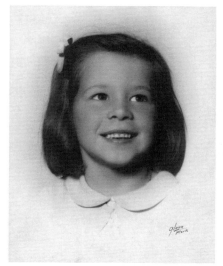

The author at six years old.

The author at eight years old (as you can see, I began falling out of trees . . . the tomboy years began).

The author at ten years old (as you can see by my hair-cut, I was trying to look like a horse with "ponytails." I guess this was a sign that I would become a jockey someday).

Alice and Jim Meglemre (Mom and Dad). My folks never said, "No, you're a girl, and girls don't ride racehorses." They were the first in line when I won a race or did Judy Garland (even at La Cage). And believe me . . . it took a lot for my Dad to hold his water until he got home. He didn't want to rub shoulders with Diana Ross, in the men's room at La Cage.

The author.

Actor Audrey Ruttan. I met Audrey while I did Judy Garland at La Cage. She has been a lifelong friend, and even though she is a very busy actor (Lady of a Thousand Faces), she always finds time for me. Now and then, I catch her on the tube or call her up to chat about the old days.

Actor Patricia Richarde, another friend I met at the Emmy's a few years ago. Patricia will be playing me in the script Garbo's Secret. taken from the chapter "Lucinda." I hope she knows what she is getting herself into.

L-R: Oscar and Grammy award winner singer/songwriter Christopher Cross, ABC News Weatherman Dallas Raines, and author. This photo was at the VIP tent, at the Toyota Celebrity Mini Grand Prix of Long Beach. Chris was my driving coach, and Dallas was trying to pick up some tips, and would up beating me that afternoon. If he wasn't such a great guy, I would have filed a complaint with the drivers committee. All kidding aside, we raised a lot of money for Long Beach-based charities. The very next year I exacted my revenge against Dallas, and beat him soundly. My many thanks to Valvoline Motor Oil Company for being my sponsor and trusting me with their great car.

Prime time Emmy-winning actor Peggy McCay, one of Cary Grant's favorite actors. She starred in a TV series based on Mr. G's movie Room for One More(co-starring Andrew Duggan). He liked her style of acting because it could fit any part. She is now starring in the daytime Emmy-winning soap opera Days Of Our Lives. I had the thrill of meeting Ms. McCay on the NBC set of Days, and am here to tell you that she has her best acting to come (do I hear cable calling)?

L-R Peggy McCay, star of the NBC Daytime Emmy award-winning series "Days of Our Lives." Soon to be seen in her own cable network series "The Peggy McCay Show." She will also be starring in the movie "Garbo's Secret," where she will be playing the legendary film star Bette Davis.

Acknowledgments

Charlie Whittingham (Trainer, deceased)—After looking through the record books, I'll always remember Charlie as a person who could always read his horses. Too bad he couldn't read people as well.

Harry Silbert (Shoe's Agent, deceased)—Harry taught me that no matter what, always run to win.

Bill Shoemaker (Jockey/Trainer)—What Charlie was to training, Bill was to riding. Horses were always easier to figure out.

Bob Benoit (P.R. Pro)—Brought the public closer to racing than anyone I ever knew.

Dan Smith (P.R., Del Mar)—The old school of racing P.R. who believes in the art of racing.

Jane Goldstein (Santa Anita Exec., retired)—A renaissance woman and a closet feminist. Born too soon, but catching up fast. One of my first role models.

Jimmy Kilroe (Dir. of Racing, deceased)—World authority on racing and life.

Millie Vessels (Former owner of Los Alamitos, deceased)—Loved racing, but could not fight off the bad guys. I think she died happy.

Betty Johnston (Owner/Breeder Mistress of Old English Rancho)—Lover of life. She encouraged my acting and never missed a show. She is a true friend and has shared her life with many people.

Bill Christine from the *LA Times*, Sports Dept.—If it is possible, I believe you love racing more then Charlie, Shoe, and I put together. Your stories about our barn made us all very proud and want to try harder. I thank you, along with all of the horse racing fans in the world.

Steve Wood (Track Man)—Don't lose your vision. We need safe racetracks.

Karl Ullman (Teamsters 495)—Kept me out of hot water and taught me to be a Teamster.

Roscoe Baker (Head Gate Man, Former Foreman to Bobby Frankel)—Thirty years of friendship, and thirty more to go.

Dick Smith (Dir. Security, Santa Anita & Head of TRPB)—Put up with my inexperience and exercised great patience knowing I was a fish out of water. He took me along slowly. Maybe that's why I lasted and stayed alive those sixteen years.

Nat Wess (GM CTBA)—A survivor. Always lands on his feet.

Dr. Kim Sprayberry (Veterinarian)—A woman with a mission and the courage to pull it off.

Lori Cain (a very dear friend)—Lori made me look at my life, and then made me put pen to paper. I guess if I had anyone to thank, or blame, for this book, it would have be Lori. She now lives up north with her husband Rick and their son Anthony. If ever I should get into trouble, I know Lori would come running. She is what friendship is all about.

Howard Koch, Sr. (Gentleman Horse Breeder/Producer)—Howard and I shared a lover for a couple of years . . . Telly's Pop. He was, above all, a great film maker but always had time to put a couple of dollars down on his favorite four-legged friend (sidekicks Marty Ritt and John Forsythe made up the handicapping dream team back then). By the way, John Forsythe gave us (Charlie Whittingham's exercise girls) the name "Charlie's Angels" long before the series took off.

Army Archerd (*Variety*)—If it was not for the support of "Mr A," I would have given up on this book a long time ago. Cary Grant once said of Army: "If he doesn't show up for work, this town would come to a grinding halt."

Liz Smith (Author/Columnist)—Thanks for keeping Hollywood honest. I know it must be a thankless, and full-time job. Your column has inspired my book to the point that I have had to search my own soul for the truth (or at least *my* truth). I loved your book . . . and yes, I believe you are a natural blond, and someday I would like to find out.

Peggy McCay (Actor)—Cary Grant once said of Peggy McCay that if he had had her under contract, he would still have been producing. He said she was such an-all around actor that she could fit any role. "She is the Agnes Moorhead of her time." Her best work is ahead of her.

Valvoline Motor Company—Thanks for letting me drive in the Grand Prix of Long Beach (Celebrity Pro/Am Race). My best finish was 2nd (three years in a row). I guess you considered me the Buffalo Bills of your racing stable. I had so much fun, and we did raise a lot of money for charity. You will always continue to be, to me, a really nice bunch of guys and gals.

The Strong Women of Goa—I know you . . . . and of you. Your lives shine for all women. For you have travelled the roads of the world, leaving red dust in your wake. Some day, I will tell your story.

Gene Fisher, Esq. and his sidekick G-Girl—Gene came out of retirement to guide me down this path of hell called publishing. He dotted all of my I's and crossed all of my T's.

All of the Trainers Who Let Me Learn on Their Horses—You guys must have been nuts!

All the Horses—That won and never "pulled" me in the morning. I love you all.

Kinko's Printing—(Kara Kupsh)—Thanks to her and her staff, "Me and Mr G" kept on schedule and got to the publisher on time. There is a place in heaven for people who still give service above and beyond the call of duty.

The Old Pioneer Hospital Gang—I learned more about friendships, the last twenty years, (hanging with you guys) then any other time in my life. You have always been there for me. If tomorrow brings criticism and ridicule, I know where I can get an empty shoulder to cry on.

Jean Nama (Educator/World Traveler)—There is always a teacher that makes you turn a corner. Jean Nama was that teacher. I guess she can now cross me off her list of students who needed help.

The Dissou's (past and present)—What can I say about the Goan half of the family. You guys really hung in there. The khana was always hot (gunpowder at times) and the polite conversation was always one-sided (Walter "Plato D"). Till the end, I know the red dust you call home will always be our bond.

Tony Brenna (novelist/journalist)—Thanks for listening, and feeding me your great wisdom. At times I know you could have strangled me (for my slow up-take). In the end your patience won out, and the book got done. Now, what color Range Rover did you say you wanted? Just kidding.

Hard Rock Cafe—(LA, Hollywood) My dear Franny, you filled my tummy with food, and my heart with love . . . see you on the set.

And to anyone who ever gave me a job. To the people who let me work at the job so I could write. The Southern California Physicians Insurance Exchange was where I wrote "Lucinda." Many thanks for the use of the copier, and to whoever left me all those free cokes. "Sales Topper" was written at St. Anne's Maternity Home—the sisters loved it. Being in security (PM) was made to order for the aspiring writer. (Since I didn't want to act, being a waiter was out of the question.)

To anyone who paid to see me do Judy (La Cage, Las Vegas, Hollywood, and Atlantic City)—if you want your money back, write in care of Mary Meglemre, whatever.

Last, but not least, to his holiness the Dalai Lama. He has led me down the path of light and has shown me what life is like on the other side. His words will always be kept in my heart. For he was the one who knew, long before me, that I would write this book.

He said, "live life now, and enjoy . . . because there's another life just around the corner to be lived." I guess what he was trying to tell me is that each life is a prelude to the next . . . do I smell a second book, or what?

The author and HH the Dalai Lama. I served as support security staff for his stays in Los Angeles. His life has been such a hard journey. It seems that men of peace always pick the hard road. I think Dick Gere is his eyes and ears in the U.S. On many occasions, I find Dick to be a very real person, and you can't say that about many people in this town. I hope he finds a lot more time to teach. I know I will be the first to sign up.